also by
Sam Millar

Short Stories

Rain
Stained Whispers
Darkness in Day
Bloody Memories
A Finding of Truth
House of the Deaf
New York
Sleeping Stones
Feasting with the Dead
The Barber
The Taste of a Lie
The Magician
Sadie
The Poison Collector

Poetry Collections

Cursing God All Drunk and Nasty
Love on Slate

DAR
SOUL

To Chris and Donna —
Thee Kellys.
Best wishes to me exiles in Canada

DARK SOULS

Sam Millar

Wynkin deWorde

2003

Published in 2003
by

Wynkin deWorde Ltd.,
PO Box 257, Tuam Road, Galway, Ireland.
e-mail: info@deworde.com

Copyright © Samuel Millar, 2003
All rights reserved.

The moral rights (paternity and integrity) as defined by the World Intellectual Property Organisation (WIPO) Copyright Treaty, Geneva 1996, of the author are asserted.

No part of this publication may be reproduced, stored in a retrieval system, or transmitted without the prior permission in writing of Wynkin deWorde Publishers. Within Ireland and European Union, exceptions are allowed in respect of any fair dealing for the purpose of research or private study, or criticism or review, as permitted under the Copyright and Related Rights Act, 2000 (Irl 28/2000) and the relevant EC Directives: 91/250/EEC, 92/100/EEC, 93/83EEC, 93/98/EEC, 96/9/EC and 2001/29/EC of the European Union.

Except in the United States, this book is sold subject to the condition that it shall not, by way of trade or otherwise, be lent, re-sold, hired out, or otherwise circulated without the publisher's prior consent in any form of binding or cover other than that in which it is published and without similar conditions, including this latter condition, being imposed on any subsequent purchaser.

A CIP catalogue record for this book is available from the British Library

ISBN: 0-9542607-6-7

Typeset by Patricia Hope, Skerries, Co. Dublin, Ireland
Cover illustration by Roger Derham.
Jacket Design by Design Direct, Galway, Ireland
Printed by Betaprint, Dublin, Ireland

All characters in this publication other than those clearly in the public domain are fictitious and any resemblance to real persons, living or dead, is purely coincidental.

Acknowledgements

There are so many people I should thank for their help to me on my journey as a writer. However, it would be impossible to name them all, so all I am left with is a huge thank you, from my heart, to each of you.

To Valerie Shortland and Roger and Brenda Derham for their help and perseverance in the preparation of this book – and for believing in me.

And loving thanks to my wife, Bernadette and our children for their patience in allowing me time to go upstairs, to finish Dark Souls.

It was a long journey, but we got there in the end.

Dedication

*Dark Souls,
I gladly dedicate to my wife,
Bernadette
and our children:
Kelly-Saoirse, Ashley-Patricia, Corey
and
never forgetting
Roxanne*

Prologue

Dominic Tranor was resting in a room he hadn't seen in years. It was filled with sunken memories and the smell of caked soap, and had the eerie feeling of a giant tape-recorder that had never been turned off, as if he had never left, all those years ago, hoping to make a name for himself as a journalist. At one time he had hoped to become a lawyer, but he had surrendered that dream one terrible night in a canvas of rust, oil and blood, in a place where screams went silent and innocence was destroyed.

Little had changed in the room. It was a shrine to him, from a mother who believed he would return to it – to her, forgiveness on his tongue. But absolution was impossible for him. If he couldn't forgive himself, how could he grant it to others? The last time he had seen her was when she stood behind his father, as he pulled away from him, fearful he would miss his flight. His father was almost crying, but she remained detached, her thoughts some place long gone to dust.

Two years later, when he received the news that her health was deteriorating, he laughed out loud, a wry and cynical grin distorting his face. "Deteriorating? That's funny, coming from a woman whose self-mutilation is as habitual as her lies," he had snorted. Besides, that same morning, he had a make-or-break interview with the editor of one of the most prominent newspapers in the city, and nothing was going to prevent that: "Certainly not you!"

How he sweated that morning in spite of the autumn chill clinging to his neck. He couldn't stop running to the toilet, contradicting the claims on the bottle's pink label of a settled stomach. And when the god-like man welcomed him on board, he floated out of the office, the rush of adrenalin giving him wings that no one could clip. No one. And most definitely not a woman who had only herself to blame, devouring 30 to 40 cigarettes each day, washing their taste away with cheap whiskey or wine.

Months after his appointment as a court reporter, a telegram arrived at Dominic's apartment, carrying with it the fierceness of an uninvited relative. He knew its origin and refused to open it for days, hiding it between books before shoving it beneath his bed, like dirty socks and grubby underwear. Finally, tearing it open angrily, one word spat at him over and over again: Dying.

He sat the telegram down and went to the window. Traffic was shimmering in the afternoon heat, all silvery and scaly, like stranded salmon captured upstream upon the rocks. He poured a large whiskey and stared through the twisted glass, turning everything amber.

Two hours and an empty bottle later, he read the hazy words telling him that she had weeks, perhaps days, and to get the next flight out.

Just like that: The Next Flight Out.

He tried to sleep but the anger in him resurfaced, gnawing at his skull. 'Who the fuck are *they* to tell *me* to return?' He fell back on the pillow, but not before reasoning with himself as to why he wouldn't be going, after all, to stare at the waxed face of his dying mother. He had seen it too many times before.

Things progressed beautifully for a while. Months of hard work and no sleep began to pay dividends. A new editor took over, eager to bring the newspaper back; back to its one-time sphere of influence. He needed new blood, people who were not afraid to go for the jugular. Dominic was perfect. A loner with bloodshot eyes and hungry with bills – plus his work on local crime bosses had impressed.

Then came the devastating news that would send him back, back to a place he neither cared for nor wished to see.

'Isn't that your hometown, where that man, Larkin Baxter killed all those people?' asked the editor, not believing his luck that someone from the same town as the murderer could be working here in the building. 'I knew from the first day I saw you at your desk, working like a beaver, that you would be an asset to the team.'

A few hours later, the plane touched down, bringing tiny bats scurrying in Dominic's stomach, making him feel like a condemned prisoner who had once escaped justice. He shook his head at the irony of it.

From the bedroom window, a breeze brought in a tribe of familiar smells, of melted tar cooling in the night and paint, newly used, its tacky wetness blending perfectly into the room's dampness. The sky rumbled and the soft breeze gathered strength. He could smell rain and mud and it stank like blood, but it was the attar of rotten apples carpeted on the ground outside which brought back school days and a desk full of untouched lunches with naked bread that made him burn with shame and humiliation.

'I shouldn't have returned,' he admonished himself, as a migraine – caused by the paint or nerves – began to drill into the area just above his eyes.

He lay back on the bed and slowly closed his eyes, waiting for the pills to do their magic. Eventually the pain slowly eased and the room stopped spinning as he forced himself to the edge of the bed, dreading the thought of all the work that lay ahead.

Reluctantly, his hand moved to the old cupboard as he took a deep breath before opening its battered door. He wondered if the folder still sat there, at the bottom of the cupboard, waiting for him? Part of him hoped it was gone, destroyed when his mother cleaned out his room; the other part – the journalist part – prayed for it to be there, make his task that little bit easier.

The smell of mothballs greeted him and he knew immediately the answer. Underneath two of his old shirts, resting in their shadow, sat the green folder and once again the mixed emotions ran through his body of finding something not really sought.

He pulled the folder from its hideout and placed it alongside an army of files and newspaper-clippings scattered throughout the room. He picked out a few pages from the folder, switched on the light at his old desk and placed them on top, selecting the least disfigured. It was a front-page article from the local rag, describing in detail a police report and Larkin Baxter's penchant for violence:

(1) *'He once threatened to wring our Paul's neck – then mine.'*
Mister Walker, a former neighbour; now living in Australia.

It was the Larkin's first taste of true publicity, and he relished it. Dominic could remember Larkin buying twenty copies of the newspaper, distributing them to his cronies, who in turn slapped him on the back and shook his hand, smiling as they congratulated him. He remembered how Larkin smiled back with that dead smile of his, seeing through their lies, knowing how they hated him. But that was okay, because they feared him. And that was what he wanted. Fear. To keep them in its arena:

(2) *'He knew everything, Larkin Baxter. He was omnipresent. You couldn't take a shit without him knowing its weight.'*
A victim.

(3) 'He instilled fear, but so subtle you hardly realised it until it was too late, touching ya right on the shoulder.'
Death-Face Charley, a rival.

(4) 'Evil. Sheer evil.'
A neighbour.

(5) 'Kind. He'd give ya his last penny. Always fed my cats. They never went hungry when he was about. . .'
Sadie, barmaid at *Jecks*.

(6) 'Loved animals…most of the time. Wouldn't hurt a fly. People? Now that's a different story.'
His cousin, Francis.

(7) 'Thought he wuz a wizard or somethin' like that. Thought he could make people disappear. I suppose, in the end, he could.'
Asked that his name not be printed.

(8) 'They asked me if I thought him an angel. Me? Can ya believe it? Me who don't even believe in God, let alone bloody angels!'
An uncle.

Dominic wanted to stop reading. Jetlag was taking its toll, but something inside drove him on, relentlessly, seeking something for himself as well as his boss. It were as if Larkin was still weaving his magic, forcing him to continue, laughing at him, knowing him just a little too well:

(9) 'Had a way with lies. You just knew he was lying through his teeth, but still you wanted to believe him. Not a liar. Just a stranger to the truth, I suppose.'
A friend, now serving three life sentences for murder.

(10) *'The tests resulted in a distorted picture. The reason being the subject's manipulative power – something that should have been spotted by a competent psychiatrist. Unfortunately, Doctor Stoppard's ineptitude and unsophisticated method prevented a clearer, more authentic report. It is now evident that the subject was fully in control of his state of consciousness, never losing voluntary power of action or thought, pretending to be highly responsive to suggestions and directions from the hypnotist.'*

    Confidential report, highly critical of the administration's doctor in Allenwood Mental Institute, who supported the release of the accused from the institute on the grounds that he believed he posed no threat to society.

(11) *'Heartbreaking. He never realised his potential, preferring to be the clown in class to win so-called friends. Boys like him never have friends; that's the price you pay when you're a genius. People look at me when I use that word to describe him. But that's exactly what he was. A genius. Yes, sir.'*

    Mr Richard N Johnson, Larkin Baxter's science teacher.

(12) *'He was an ugly baby, something terribly . . . odd about him. His tiny eyes held sinister knots of anger and were opened from day one. He even had teeth, God the night!'*

    Nurse Alice, midwife.

(13) *'I hated that boy from the moment he was born, tearing out of me with those bloody little hands, ripping me in half, entering the world with a grin, all bloody and shit. My anger of him was equal to Eden's God. Anger, that over the years, turned to unadulterated hate. It wasn't my fault what he turned out to be. Blame God. He created the monster.'*

    His mother, Gail.

Each report Dominic read conjured up images he had tried

to suppress. He had attempted, and failed, to erase not only the town, but specifically Larkin and Dakota.

Abruptly, his thoughts were interrupted by his father's voice coming from the living room, below. He could hear another voice mingling with it, almost in a whisper, like a confessional.

Or a conspiracy, he thought bitterly, smiling at his paranoia. *Probably some fuckin' nosey neighbour enquiring about me, asking how I've been, as if they really care. This fuckin' town, this fuckin' weasel and its offspring. I hate you all.*

As he closed the folder, a photo fell from its centre, tumbling in slow motion towards the carpet. He bent and picked it up, studying a memory in black and white, of three kids smiling for the camera.

What actors, he thought. *All anyone had to do was look at those terrible eyes and mouths with their exquisite nastiness of shadows, to realise the smiles were lies, washed then hidden.*

He sat the picture down and thought about burning it but looked again at the faces: Two boys. One girl. All locked together like rust on iron. One of the boys has a wizard's hat on. He's winking. The girl is pretending to strangle the wizard. *Is she really pretending?* The other boy in the picture seems quite lost, embarrassed to be posing with the other two.

You haven't changed much, have you? thought Dominic, glancing from photo to reflection in the mirror. *Some grey here, face a little fuller.* He wondered how the other two looked, what the years had done to them. *If only we had never met, if only we had remained the loners we were meant to be. If only we had never killed. If only . . .*

He rubbed his eyes and placed his work on the table. He wouldn't need any pills tonight. He would sleep – if sleep it could be called – but the nightmare would still be waiting for him, smiling. It always waited . . .

Chapter One

From his house, Larkin Baxter watched as an angry wind raged against the old shop across the street. At one time, the shop had contained statues and religious pictures of God with angry angels defeating Satan's fiery army: Good versus Evil, Light fighting Dark.

Larkin remembered one of the paintings, wondering if it truly would be like that, in the end? Or did the Devil have another trick up his sleeve?

They were fascinating pictures – if only for the laughable parody of pain-faced angels defeating gnashing, hairy devils whose faces, uncannily, resembled the one-time owner of the shop, Mister Rootree, a miserable old man who died a lonely but quite peaceful death in bed, one Friday night, two hours after shrouding the shop in darkness by removing all the light bulbs from their housing. It were as if the old man had realised that surrounding himself with God did not necessarily mean he was heading in that direction.

Larkin had always loved the solitary feel of the old

abandoned place with its fearful loneliness avoided by others, but now he hated it.

It had always been derelict – at least as far back as he could remember. Pigeons made their home in it, as did rats and the stray, wild cats that spat and chased the dogs, leaving their snouts a bloody mess.

He remembered – hating to remember – how he had climbed in through the back window, searching for something he knew couldn't be there. The dark drew him in, seducing with its magnetic pull, knowing the weakness and curiosity that the young possess. The shop always seemed to be covered in a darkness that never really left. For the majority of the day, shadows overlapped the sunlight that tried to slip in through the windows. A decapitated statue of some saint lay languishing in a corner, mottled with age and dung. Webs of silk and dust covered a village of cigarette butts that lay scattered on the floor, like empty shells from a war.

The smell of human waste was overpowering as he moved from room to room, and as his eyes adjusted in the dull interior of the last room, to his horror the floor was carpeted by the carcasses of dead birds, their fragile bones gleaming like hulls from tiny ships caught in rocks, each blending wickedly into an origami of shadows and repulsiveness.

The ever-skilful rats had been proficient in stripping the flesh. It was a massacre, a feasting of the dead, and he was baffled how creatures of flight could have been captured so easily.

Only when he stumbled on the two birds, each crucified to the beams, their necks twisted into grotesque, feathered question marks, did he realise the rats had only played a meagre part in the bloody pantomime.

A shudder iced his spine. What if the killer was still in the shop, watching him this minute, knife in hand? No one would know. No one had seen him enter. The killer would leave him dying in his own blood, just like the ugly birds pinioned to the wood, staring at him in disbelief at his stupidity in remaining. Finally, the rats would come, finishing the job, taking his face first . . .

The shop's acoustics echoed behind him in the darkness, making his heart thump and his face swell with rushing blood. He wanted to ask who was there but feared it would expose him, so he moved carefully across the room, as if swimming in wet sand.

If he could only make it another few feet, freedom would sweep him away to safety, away from whatever lurked there, watching him, ready to gut and slice.

Suddenly, the sound of feet crushing glass made his hair tight, burning his scalp. Liquid was flooding his brain and he could no longer think. Was it *his* feet, or someone else's that had made the sound?

He heard a laugh, so soft it was almost silent, meant for his ears only: sinister and deliberate. It rendered him motionless, like the stillness of an ice sculpture as his heart threatened to explode in his skull. What if it were Mister Rootree's ghost?

Not thinking, not caring, he took a chance and ran. He had only one thought and that was to escape. He wouldn't die: Not here with the dead.

Slowly, the intense, claustrophobic blackness began to shift, almost imperceptibly, into dull strings of coloured lights as he neared his only hope of escape, the span of which now confused and infuriated him by its utter unfamiliarity.

It was funny how John Wayne always made it look so easy, jumping through windows of a saloon as the bad guys shot at him. But, he wasn't the Duke. He was a failure, and the perfect casement of glass suddenly became a kaleidoscopic pattern, all in slow motion, as he tumbled to the ground watching his blood hit it before he did, the shreds of glass following him, piercing every inch of skin on his face.

Afterwards, he could only remember the pain as he drifted in and out of needle-induced nightmares, screaming for water to be thrown on his face to stop the burning heat that came from it.

People with masks floated above him, surrounding the face of his mother. *"Scarred for life"*, he remembered her voice whispering, contradicting the specialist who sat in the fat leather chair, manipulating the shadows on his face, obscuring clarity of expression.

"They will fade. Given time, he'll hardly notice them" proclaimed the specialist, reciting a line he had used many times before, his face a politician's on polling day.

But years went and there had been no fading – either of scars or memory. If anything, the opposite was true.

He would have gone insane had it not been for the comfort and friendship of the *Werewolf, Dracula* and *Frankenstein*. The plastic monsters were the only therapy he needed, not doctors, not liars with their perfect words. The monsters helped sustain him, building his confidence as he meticulously attached each intricate and tiny piece, shaping them, granting life to them. At night, with the lights dead, they glowed eerily, like lighthouses bathed in fog, guarding him against the completeness of isolation.

As the wind calmed, settling for the night, his thoughts turned to Monday and school. He hated school. Actually, he enjoyed school; he only hated the people in it. The teachers and pupils regarded him as a freak. He could see the loathing in their eyes, regardless of how much their faces tried to pretend.

He was good at reading eyes. Months of agonising therapy and perpetual skin grafts had honed this tiny yet significant gift. He loved it when people lied, pretending they were comfortable in his company. He could almost smell their fear and guilt, their sickening pathetic pity and silent prayers to their God, thanking Him that they didn't have the horrible useless face.

They couldn't endure for a week what their God had forced

him to live with for the rest of his life. But that was fine. He was stronger than all of them – more powerful than their God.

'Time will prove it,' he whispered, making his way downstairs, avoiding the creaking floorboard directly outside his mother's room. The squeaky wood was only one of many traps set by her. Rusted door handles played their part, as did the lights with their spitting electrical tongues hissing like snakes in the night.

But he was more than a match for her, more than a match for her warped ingenuity.

He couldn't help smiling as he slipped away from her door, her soft snores of exhaustion following him like angry bugs de-winged and encased in glass as he made his way towards the fridge in the shop.

Opening the fridge, he pushed back the ice-cream and chocolate lollypops before tunnelling under the secret compartment of ice, watching as the brown paper bag revealed itself.

Slowly he removed the bag and smiled. For the first time in months, he was looking forward to Monday and school.

Chapter Two

Dominic Tranor made his way towards the crumbling handball alley at the back of the school. The alley was the hub and centre of all things that truly ruled the pupils of Archangel Secondary School, where the *real* lessons in life prevailed: card games that relieved you of dinner money and bus fare home; bullies who demanded – and received – payment for protection; where magazines of naked women playing volley ball could be looked at for five minutes at a time – all for the price of a bar of chocolate.

Sometimes just entering the alley took tremendous courage. A wrong look at the wrong person at the wrong time could have altering and devastating affects – usually on the face. Yet, not to be seen there meant cowardice, granting every would-be and up-and-coming thug a chance to enhance his own reputation by hunting you down after school.

The consequences of a no-show far outweighed the bubbling acid in Dominic's stomach. It was better to face the hyenas; though not everyone dared – and not everyone wanted to face the King of the Hyenas, Nutter Brown; a hard case whose reputation for inflicting violence was legendary.

Nutter had been expelled for a brutal assault on a teacher, but his banishment was short-lived after a visit from Nutter's father and two ape-like uncles to "persuade" the headmaster to give the boy a second chance. The headmaster – a lover and owner of three pedigree dogs – was handed a video tape of *The Godfather*, and told to pay particular attention to what was found in the bed of the reluctant film director.

Two days later Nutter was back, his reputation strengthened, his violence more vicious than ever. He was untouchable and everyone in school knew it.

Dominic walked the customary circle of death before making his way, tentatively, up the side steps towards the back entrance of the assembly hall, each step bringing him closer to freedom, each step releasing a tiny pocket of air from his lungs. He knew they were watching him, watching for that nervous twitch to the face that betrayed and screamed out loud. He could feel the eyes burning on him as he walked further and further, counting each step in a whisper. *Eight more. Seven . . .*

He knew the eyes burning the back of his head belonged to Nutter and he tried to calm himself. He had his dinner money – a good bargaining chip – but would it be enough? Perhaps Nutter would simply take the money then beat the crap out of him anyway, just for the fun of it, just for being Dominic Shit-the-Pants Tranor.

When the hand touched his shoulder, Dominic jumped inches off the ground, almost falling back down the steps.

'I've still got my dinner money, Nutter, and tomorrow I'll . . .' His fear quickly turned to anger seeing the owner of the hand. 'What the fuck are you doing, sneakin' the fuck up on me! I don't even know you, and you've the cheek to touch me with everyone watchin'.'

The owner of the hand was Larkin, a strange kid who normally walked about the school as if in a trance. His scarred face had a menacing look and this got him a free passage from the hyenas. Rumour had it he had killed a boy in another school, a boy who had inflicted the scars. Others said acid had been poured on his face by his mad mother who owned a shop in town, but rarely opened it due to her 'illness' – at least that's what the cardboard notice claimed; everyone else said too much cheap wine.

Whatever the truth about Larkin, he had become like Nutter – untouchable.

Larkin rarely communicated with anyone, always avoiding, so Dominic was more than surprised when he whispered, 'I've somethin' to show you. Meet me in Billy Ryan's, after school.' He kept glancing over his shoulder, suspiciously, his dark eyes becoming tiny slits.

Before Dominic could say no, Larkin was gone, running defiantly down the steps, back down to the jungle towards the hyenas and other prowling animals, as if daring them to attack him.

Dominic quickly glanced about, hoping no one had spotted them talking. *If* he decided to go to Billy Ryan's, it would be to let Larkin know never *ever* to come near him again. He had enough problems at home. The less he had here, the better.

Quickly, he opened the assembly door and slithered in, welcoming its quietness and false security. Ten seconds later he was rushing down the corridor, panicking, heading for the toilet as the fear-factor kicked in. He was touching cloth and wondered if he would make it?

Billy Ryan's was an old dilapidated house that was used by all the kids in the surrounding streets as a hideout. It was a citadel, a place where all the cares of being a kid were ancient history; a place that never let you down, screamed or lost its temper, beat or criticised. It was everything all the kids wanted at home and despite their youth all understood it was something that would not last. They were forced to drink it as quickly as possible before it became only a memory, before it became like them: full of flaws and pockmarked with doubts.

It was a good ten minutes later – a lifetime in Dominic's eyes – when Larkin finally arrived, his face glistening with sweat.

'You've kept me waitin' all day,' Dominic accused.

Larkin said nothing as he fumbled in a navy-blue bag, the type Fleming, the greengrocer used to store onions. The blue was almost black, caused by seeping liquid.

The old house always had those strange smells ghosting in and out of it, of dampness and dust mingling with urine and shit, but this was an altogether alien stench oozing menacingly from the bag.

'Fuck . . . What is it?' Dominic moved away from the bag, fearful of the reply.

'What d'ya think it is?' Larkin was smiling a strange smile, one that belonged to a corpse. 'Have a guess. Go on.'

Dominic didn't want to have a guess. He wanted to be in his own house, away from here, away from this strange boy with the jigsaw face and its savage lines.

'It looks like somethin' in *Bannon's* window,' replied Dominic, his throat tight. Bannon was the local butcher.

'Close, but no cigar. Take a better look,' insisted Larkin, pushing it under Dominic's nose.

The smell was terrible. It made Dominic think of an aunt who had died, stretched out in her coffin all those years ago.

'Get it away from me. I mean it. Take it away. *Now!*'

'Guess,' insisted Larkin, almost spitting in Dominic's face, opening the bag even wider.

Gingerly, Dominic peered inside and quickly realised the terrible content, knew what it was. He'd seen a picture of one in an encyclopaedia in school. The picture both frightened and fascinated him, branding his memory with its white-hot horror.

'It's a foetus. Just like the one in the science book,' glared Dominic. 'Are you satisfied?'

A puzzle look appeared on Larkin's face. 'A what? Don't be stupid. Where would I get one of those? It's a foot,' he replied, calmly without a care in the world, as if carrying a foot in a bag was the most natural thing. 'Good job we don't have a science test tomorrow. Old Johnson would take a buckle in his eye if he thought you couldn't tell the difference between a baby and a foot.'

He was laughing now; not at Dominic, but some dark secret that had yet to be told.

Seeing the door ajar, Dominic thought about making a run for it, get the hell away. But he didn't run, as the morbid curiosity of youth outweighed the sensible alternative.

In the ice, encased like a fish from the fishmonger's window, was a foot, almost perfect except for the missing big toe. Dominic laughed with nerves, relieved it was 'only' a foot, not a dead baby.

'Where did you get it?'

'Haven't you figured it out? Last month? Down at *Copper's*?'

'*Copper's*?' Then it came to him. 'The gas explosion?'

'Yes. Two men dead, four injured,' replied Larkin, imitating a news-flash voice. 'Would you look at the dirt under the nails? He must never have washed himself, the dirty pig.' Larkin held the foot by the icy heel, angling it so that the dusty sliver of sun sneaking through the window captured it in all its horrible loathsomeness. The foot looked as if it were trying to break free from its icy prison, kick Dominic in the teeth, run away.

'What are you doin' runnin' about the place with it? Shouldn't you give it to the priest or someone?' asked Dominic.

'The priest?' Larkin's eyes tightened. 'Hasn't he enough power over people? Fuck him. I would never trust that bastard. He's got more tongues than the Holy Ghost. Besides, this is one piece of power *I'm* keepin'.' He looked into Dominic's eyes trying to read his thoughts on what he intended to do.

The sensible thing for Dominic would have been to tell his mother – or at least a schoolteacher, but the way Larkin looked at him exorcised all acts of betrayal from his mind and caused tiny sparks to camp at the edge of his neck, biting and burning.

'Where have you kept it, all this time? The explosion was over a month ago.'

'I hid it. In our fridge, at the shop,' he replied, returning the trophy to the bag. The smell of dead onions and putrid meat had now taken over the room.

'In the shop? In the fridge with all the ice pops and ice cream?'

'Yes,' replied Larkin, nonchalant.

Dominic's stomach churned. 'You bastard! I bought a *Strawberry-Joker* from your ma's shop last week. That foot was probably stuck to it. How the hell did she not see it' he asked, knowing it was her "illness" that was to blame. 'Full of bloody wine, probably.'

Dominic would never forget that look on Larkin's face, something terrible and indescribable at that exact moment as he stared at him, his eyes burning like embers. Years later he would remember that look as the glare of a killer weighing up in a split second how he deemed to dispose of a body.

Larkin said nothing as he turned his back, exiting with the bag dangling to his side, leaving Dominic staring into the darkness.

Chapter Three

The waterfall was coming straight at Dominic as he waited for the inevitable. Within seconds, he was gasping for air as his head went under, his body heavy, anchoring him to the filthy bottom of Jackson Lake. Someone had tied his hands and feet and he was powerless as water flooded his mouth, choking him.

His last mental picture was of his younger brother, Timmy, laughing, throwing more water into the lake. Larkin was there, also, dangling a smelly, rotten foot in front of his face.

Drenched in sweat, Dominic awoke, struggling with the bedclothes like a wrestler gone mad. Within seconds, he was free and the room steadied as he gasped for air. The nightmare was over and he smiled to himself with the satisfaction of a survivor.

But the smile froze just as quickly once he realised it wasn't sweat he was drenched with.

'Ma! He's done it again!' Dominic's distressed voice broke the settled calm of an early morning; a morning that should have seen his mother get a bit of a "lay on" until 6.00, when she would prepare for the lodgers' breakfast.

A few minutes later his mother's haggard face appeared at the doorway of his room.

'Can you not shout a wee bit harder, dear,' said her edgy, sarcastic voice. 'Maggie Bentley, two streets away, can't hear you. I'm sure you've disturbed Mister Kane and Mister Costa.'

'But, Ma . . . he's done it again. Pissed all over me.'

'*Listen, you* . . .' she whispered, quietly but with venom in her voice. 'Have I not warned you about using such language in the house – or *anywhere*?'

'Look at the state of me –'

'Did you understand a word I said?'

'Yes . . .'

His mother turned to her younger son. 'Now, Timmy, what were you told about going to bed without doing a wee first? There's no excuse for a big boy, almost twelve, doing this.'

She reached and pulled the wet vest from Timmy who was oblivious of his actions, saying nothing in his own defence.

When he was nine, Timmy fell from the back of the coalman's lorry, smashing his skull. He was never the same after that and sporadically wet the bed – and Dominic – at least three to four times a week.

'Just give him time,' said his mother, when it first happened. 'He'll stop, once he's healed.'

But that was little comfort to Dominic who was getting dog's abuse at school over the smell of his brother's urine. Besides, it had been almost three years since the accident. *When* would he stop?

Pushing himself out of bed, Dominic crept down the stairs like a ham actor, just for the benefit of his mother's gaze on his back. He knew the lodgers were wide-awake as he listened to the choking cough they made, as if sending out secret messages to each other, just like the apes did in *Tarzan*.

Dominic hated the lodgers. They were a perpetual reminder of how poor his mother and father really were; how they had never made a penny from them and perpetually in debt because of them – his mother's battered purse held testimony to that. It was a fat, working-class purse, swelling like the bellies of starving children, fat with the pain of IOUs and pawn tickets.

His mother, Julia, was a workaholic, scrubbing and cleaning and always smelling of *Daz*, bleach and carbolic soap. The soap stained her hands the colour of raw wounds.

His father, John, worked the boats, six days a week at sea, cleaning out the oil drums that accumulated in giant heaps in their hulls. He only got the job because no one else would take it.

Dominic could never remember a time when his father didn't smell of oil, or when his skin was ever clean. The oil seemed to have cast a perpetual shadow on him and no amount of scrubbing in the back of the house would erase it.

Initially, Dominic thought his mother hated using the coarse brush with its porcupine quills, which left his father's back bloody and scarred with evil looking whiplash-like marks. But as the years progressed and the seeping bitterness cemented, Dominic sensed she secretly enjoyed it, punishing his father for their misery and his lack of ambition and skill.

'You deserve every bit of this,' Dominic remembered hearing her whisper one Saturday night as she dug the brush deep into his father's skin, tearing it with bloody scratches. Sitting in dirty water like some pathetic monk offering up his suffering to God.'

Deep down, Dominic was ashamed of his father's muted acceptance of his mother's scorpion tongue. He wished his father to be more like the other kids' fathers who were unemployed but at least managed to stay clean. *I'll never be dirty in my life*, he vowed to himself. *Even if it means starving to death, my pockets empty, I'll never let oil touch me.*

Dominic hated the smell of oil, almost as much as he hated Mister Cecil Kane, the evil-smelling and foul-mouthed lodger who was full of drunken farts and marbled spit. Dominic dreaded any contact with Kane who had a tendency to slap him

'Why'd you do that for?' asked a bewildered Dominic, rubbing the back of his head, the first time it happened. 'I didn't do nothin' to you, did I?'

Kane glared at him. 'All dirty children are up to somethin'. That's just in case. And here's another one, for good measure.' *Whack!*

That was why, every night without fail, Dominic prayed for the death of Kane. Not just a simple death, but a terrifying bloody death, his body all mangled beyond recognition before he was sent straight to Hell. Wouldn't that be something? That old bastard in the ground, where he belongs, worms burrowing out his hairy nose and fart box?

'Can't you just get rid of him, Ma?' asked Dominic, at breakfast. 'I hate him. He smells like stink-bombs and always slaps me for nothin'.'

'And who would be worried about you hating them? And what's wrong with a bit of slapping? You probably deserved it,' stated his mother, glaring at him as she placed a piece of bread on his plate. 'Mister Kane brings money to this house, and until the day you start to earn your keep, you'll eat up and shut up. If anyone is getting kicked out of here, it'll be your useless father. Now stop annoying me, or you'll be on the list as well.' She turned and left.

In the back kitchen, she drank some water to calm herself down. 'Selfish and useless! The whole lot of them,' she mumbled. 'Think it's easy, running this shit-hole?' She peeped through the kitchen curtain at her son, who munched on the toast, unaware of her eyes. 'Sitting there, eating my food, criticising. The cheek of it.'

She reflected grimly, how she had captured Kane that particular day, all those years ago. He was no prize catch, but beggars couldn't be choosers. And that was what she had almost become: a beggar.

She was feeling more depressed than usual, that wet afternoon. A scoundrel by the name of Keever had upped and disappeared into the night, owing her four weeks of food and rent. She needed the vacant room filled, and quickly set about putting her plan into action – a plan she knew carried no guarantee of success.

Upon reaching the barbershop, she stood for a few seconds and fixed her hair in the window's reflection. Satisfied at her appearance, she opened the door and coughed, alerting the barber – who was engrossed in conversation – to her presence. 'If I could have a minute of your time, Mister Kane,' she said, awkwardly. 'I would like to discuss some business with you – that is, when you're finished at the shop, today.'

Kane was surprised to see her face at the door. It was a novelty, a woman in his barbershop.

'Yes . . . of course, Missus Tranor. But can I be of help now? Friday is my busiest day.'

Six customers turned their heads in unison, waiting her reply.

'No, Mister Kane. Too many mouths and noses,' she replied, glaring at the men who quickly turned their attention to the newspapers and magazines resting in their fingers. 'You know my address. I'll expect you shortly after six. Good day.'

Later that night, intrigued, Kane knocked on the door of the house. It was two minutes after six.

'First things first, Mister Kane,' said Julia Tranor, ushering him in quickly. The less the neighbours knew of her plans, the better for all. 'I've prepared some hot supper for you. I'm sure you must be famished, working away all day, not a break'

No, please, don't go to any bother for me. I had some sandwiches and –'

'Sandwiches? A man eating *sandwiches*?' A false look of revulsion appeared on her face. 'That's terrible, Mister Kane, you poor man. Now, let me take your coat while you sit yourself down and enjoy those sausages and roast spuds. They'll do you the world of good. You'll not find better cooking anywhere, if I say so myself.'

Julia allowed Kane to sit and quietly devour the food. Each mouthful was calculated by the woman's keen mind. This was an expensive meal and she knew her gamble had better pay off. She thought about offering him a tiny brandy, which she had hidden for special occasions, but thought better of it. He might look upon her as a drunk and her plan would be in tatters.

'That was delicious, Missus Tranor,' said Kane, pushing the plate away, twenty minutes later. 'I haven't had a meal like that since Mary . . .' His voice drifted off.

Julia placed her hand on Kane's shoulder, squeezing it slightly. 'You're with friends now, Mister Kane. No need for embarrassment. We all know how much you miss your dear wife and what a tragedy it must have been for you, last year.'

Kane nodded solemnly. He hadn't spoken to anyone since Mary's death, about how lonely he had become, how he dreaded going home to an empty house.

'Yes, it has been hard . . .'

She wondered if the brandy should be produced, but decided against it. *Not yet*, she reasoned. *Timing is crucial.*

'Well, Mister Kane, I've a proposition to make to you – one that should be beneficial to both of us.' She smiled, hating its necessity. 'As you may be aware, I now have a vacant room – the best in the house, I should add – and I want you to see it for yourself, tell me what you think, before I advertise in the newspaper, tomorrow.'

Before Kane could reply, she gently but firmly took his elbow and guided him upstairs and into the room.

A massive fire was burning with logs crackling and spitting. An old wireless whispered in the corner with the sound of Glen Miller.

She smiled to herself. *The logs will do the trick.*

'Before you say a word, allow me to show you the view, Mister Kane. It can be quite impressive at this time of night.' She pulled back the curtains, exposing the city in all its splendour. 'You can even see City Hall from here. Look there, over to your right.'

Kane stared out at the great cranes dominating the city's skyline, standing there like enormous sentinels on duty. People were going home – thousands of them – rushing and shouting, tiny insect-people moving as one vast, blurred colour, swaying in slow motion, and going nowhere fast in the spreading darkness.

Kane could only see their heads, but that was all he wanted to see: heads, all hairy and money-potential. Julia stood beside him and he could smell the faint whiff of perfume. He swore it was *Blue Swan*, the type Mary loved to wear, and for a split second, Mary stood in the room with him, telling him what a lovely place it was.

'Now, Mister Kane, this is how I see it but I could be wrong. If so, please correct me. I see a man – a good, hardworking man – a man that should be able to come home to good food, a warm fire, a bed made with fresh clean sheets. A man that shouldn't have to travel five miles to his business and five miles back to his empty cottage, to eat alone, when he knows deep down that his good wife would turn in her grave to see him so unhappy.' She watched his reaction, but his face surrendered nothing. Irritated, she continued, 'I'm sure she would tell you to do the right thing. Sell the house, move in with this family, knowing that for the rest of your life you will be well taken care of. I know you've only been in our town a few years, but you are like one of the family to us all.'

God, she couldn't believe how well she had said that wee speech! She only wrote it yesterday, practising and practising. She almost believed it herself. But was it enough? Had she convinced *him*?

She could almost taste the victory, yet still the hesitancy sounded in his voice.

'You're far too kind, Missus Tranor, but it's something I'll have to sleep on. Perhaps tomorrow, if that would be fine by you?'

No, it was anything but fine. Tomorrow would bring a clear

head and a cold judgement. She needed that agreement tonight.

She reached and brought the brandy up from behind the seat. 'Certainly, Mister Kane, but I can't allow myself to permit you to leave on a terrible night like this, without something to warm your insides.' She walked to the tiny cupboard and produced two glasses. '*Hennessy*, Mister Kane. Nothing but the best for my lodgers.'

Julia watched as Kane's withered lips manoeuvred on the glass, the hairy nostrils flaring at the aroma, the Adam's apple bobbing up and down as it protruded from his skinny shrunken neck.

I've lost him, she thought, as the brandy disappeared quickly down his eager throat. *I pushed him too far – too quickly. He knows what I'm up to.*

The heat of the room was taking its toll on Kane as the brandy pumped through his veins. He loved that sensation. He wanted another glass, but wondered if it would be rude to ask?

'I must sit down for a moment, Missus Tranor. My feet seem light – as does my head. It must be the heat from the fire. Please forgive me.'

'Don't be silly. You're with friends.' She quickly placed a pillow against his back before reaching for the bottle. 'Allow me to fill your glass. And please, call me Julia.'

There was that smell again, he thought, as she pressed tightly against him, *the* Blue Swan *smell*. The room was moving strangely and he thought he saw his wife's eyes staring into his.

'Are you okay, Mister Kane?' asked Julia, her face an inch from his.

He could see an inch of her cleavage. It was lovely. 'Cecil. Please, call me Cecil . . . Julia. And yes, I certainly am okay. Perfectly okay.' Smiling, he reached and touched her face. 'If it's fine by you, Julia, I *would* like to stay the night . . .'

She could have kissed the old goat. God knows she was prepared to go further, if necessary. Instead, she helped him into bed, extinguishing the light before she left, grateful she wasn't touching his body – at least not this night.

Chapter Four

Over the coming weeks, Larkin showed the foot to a select few. Occasionally, he permitted an audience in his bedroom, practically becoming a head-of-state. He *had* been right all along. The foot *was* power, and the kids' eyes – those betraying mirrors of the soul – reflected back to him their fears, repulsiveness and infatuation with something long dead, but like magic and Lazarus had been brought back to life by him.

'You're a bloody magician, Larkin. Know that?' enthused one of the kids. 'A bloody magician.'

They all agreed. *A bloody magician.*

Magician. The word itself meant magic, and magic it became. Magician. The word ballooned in his brain, swelling it, intoxicating it with all the possibilities that he never thought possible. He whispered it, to himself, an invisible chant, savouring its sound on his lips, feeling the skin tightening on his face, changing that scarred face forever, as if he had drunk a magic potion. Magic. Magic. Magic . . . He knew all along he had been a magician, but to hear it from the crowd meant so much more.

From that moment – hearing those words of approval from people who normally wouldn't be seen dead with him – Larkin reinvented body and soul as the feeling of power surged through blood and bone. He was *Magician,* a force; an unstoppable force and God help anyone who tried to stop him. From here on, he would sharpen his power to become the most powerful magician ever. If it took a lifetime – so be it. His power would be fear, and he would learn to harvest its full potential.

Soon, Larkin was learning every trick from old magic books bought second-hand down at the local flea market. He made coins appear from ears and noses and turned metal bars into rubbery snakes before progressing to more incredible stunts such as turning birds into yellow and blue silk, making them disappear with a click of his magic wand. Later – much later – he would master even more profound tricks by making people disappear, though not into silk, and not in a nice way: No, not in a nice way at all.

He would always remember that phrase people said about him: *Wouldn't be seen dead with that weirdo.* Years later, he would smile at that. Some of them *would* be seen with him – very much dead.

Chapter Five

It was the middle of June, when Dominic decided to go skinny-dipping in Jackson Lake, a stretch of water barely one mile from where he lived. The lake could be deceptively still at times, but when it suited, it could be crafty in its nature, lassoing the unwary with a ripple.

The summer – for Dominic – always seemed to clog the pores with youthful expectation, of *Mister Softy* tunes floating thickly in the heat and of dogs panting in withered shadows. But more importantly, school was gone forever – or at least for ten weeks.

As he removed his shoes, the early morning heat became oppressive and the biting bugs deadly. But the bugs could never be as deadly as the snakes that supposedly hid in the black muck in Jackson Lake, waiting for their chance. No one had ever witnessed one skinny snake, but that didn't prevent people from believing.

Dominic tried to convince himself that he never fully believed that snakes actually lived in the water, but nagging doubts always made him cautious each time he entered. Deep down, this added to the thrill, wondering when those ever-staring eyes would suddenly appear, inches from his face, before ripping it in half.

He always used the west side of the lake, where the water was clearer yet colder. The east side of the lake was no longer used by anyone, after the Joey Maxwell incident, two summers back. Dominic would never forget that day – no one who witnessed it would.

Some of the kids rested on the grassy knoll, that hot Thursday afternoon, sipping on bottles of beer stolen from the back door of *Gino's,* eating greasy sandwiches and hotdogs. Everyone was in good form. School was finished, and even the usual collection of misfits and bullies were mute with contentment as the sun baked down, lancing out the memories of maths and science and their impossible combination.

How long Joey Maxwell had been standing there watching, no one would know. It seemed everyone had noticed him at the exact same moment, as if he had suddenly dropped in from the sky.

Joey had always been the town clown. A dare would see him do almost anything. A double-dare and away he'd charge, into danger, immune to the consequences.

Everyone liked him – even the hyenas tolerated him.

'There's Joey!' shouted Nutter, waving an empty beer bottle in his direction. 'Gonna do a dare for us, Joey? Catch a couple of snakes for dinner?'

The entire gang laughed.

'Yea, Joey! How about some nice snake steaks for you and your da's dinner!' someone shouted, bringing more false laughter. Joey's father was a prison guard and detested by everyone in town. Quite a few of the men in town had seen the inside of the local jail, and were not impressed by the man's behaviour.

Normally, Joey would have smiled right back before plunging into the water, emerging with an old tire, pretending it was strangling the life out of him. But ever since his brother had died, three months back, Joey had changed from a boisterous good-humoured boy to a brooding recluse.

The sun had just emerged from a cloud when Joey made a slight movement with his hand. Some people said it was Joey fixing his hair; others thought it resembled a wave. Perhaps he was stopping the sun from burning his eyes?

The answer would remain a mystery as Joey, without warning, walked towards the lake, zombie-like in his speed, while the crowd on the grassy knoll, cheered him on, fearful yet enjoying every deliciously fear-charged moment of entertainment.

They screamed out the seconds, daring him to break the all-time record of one minute and ten seconds for staying under the water. '59, 60, 61, 62 . . .'

On and on they counted, their voices rising.

As they passed 70, some of the voices filtered out, slowly bringing the others with them. Initially, they all thought the silence was Joey adding to the drama. Only when the bubbles stopped surfacing did panic set in.

'Someone dive in there, see what he's up to,' commanded Nutter, panicking, knowing he might be held accountable for Joey's idiotic action. Nutter would give Joey a good kicking, just for making him look concerned in front of the gang.

But not one person moved. No one wanted to be a part of anything that might have happened under that dirty water, even though they knew it was Joey simply winding them up. Shit, he was probably away downstream, emerging over near Garrison Gardens. Double shit, he was probably watching them now, laughing his balls off at all their faces.

'Didn't any of you scum bags hear me? I said dive the fuck in there, and find out what that little fuck is up to.'

Their fear of Nutter was not as terrible as their fear of the lake – what it would reveal to them. No one moved, even though they knew the penalty of disobedience.

Dominic slithered into the shadows, thankful for once in his life that he wasn't part of Nutter's gang. His stomach told him

Joey Maxwell was down there, fish already tasting his face, peeling off his skin with their tiny teeth.

Before Nutter could pick a "volunteer", a police car pulled up, alerted by complaints from neighbours.

Immediately, one of the cops jumped into the lake, causing all the black muck to rise as he struggled to find Joey. The lake resembled one giant oil spill each time the cop emerged, shaking his head with defeat.

It took volunteers almost 40 minutes to find Joey. It took them another hour to bring his body to the surface.

Joey had handcuffed himself to the steering wheel of an old Ford that was supposed to have been brought to the surface several months before. The local council had haggled over the price, and as most things go, the wreck was quickly forgotten about. Now they had no other option.

The salvage company extracted the rusted piece of junk – with Joey attached to it like a magnet.

All who witnessed that sight would never forget it, even though they made fun about how Joey looked like Superman flying into the sky, punching a meteorite that had threatened earth.

A debilitated, half-hearted fence was quickly constructed on all sides of the lake to discourage people from using it because on a day of clear water, one might still divine a form of a boy, a sad smile on his young face, resting on the lake's sandy carpet. And while this terrifying caveat worked for most of the boys, it failed to deter Dominic. The lake was the only cooling place he had, the only excitement, the only escape from a claustrophobic home, and he wasn't for surrendering it to anyone, least of all to a ghost of a stupid dead boy.

A sense of silence, reinforced by the heat's density, settled all about Dominic. As he swam, something slipped across his peripheral vision. He stared at the thin line between the water and the sky, deep beyond the lake's fringe. Someone –

something – stared at him from the trees' shadows and suddenly he no longer felt so arrogantly brave.

His mind began to play tricks on him and he felt a coldness touch him. Was that Joey? It looked a bit like him. No one else was about. Perfect for a ghost appearing.

The water was no longer warm as his stomach made strange nervous sounds. *'I'm not shittin' myself,'* he whispered. *'I'm not afraid of anythin'. So fuck off, Joey. Go and haunt someone else.'*

Dominic wondered how long it would take for him to reach the rocky bank, grab his clothes and run like hell; wondered if he should simply forget the clothes and run home through the town, bare-hole naked?

Stop this, he told himself, *if it were Joey he wouldn't harm you. He always liked you, didn't he? Yes, me and Joey got on well, even if I did make fun of his da a few times.*

'Joey? Joey, is that you?' Dominic inched his way forward. A few more feet and he'd have his clothes.

Then, realising that this wasn't Joey back to kill him, the anger in him boiled.

'Hey, pervert!' he shouted. 'Do ya like watchin'?'

The figure emerged from the shadows, walking towards him, defiantly. At first, he thought it was one of the local kids with the crapped-in hair and beat-up Levis. Then, to his horror, he realised it was a girl.

'Who would want to look at you?' said her voice, snidely. 'Swimmin' in the west side? Scared Joey is gonna get you, little boy?'

Two seconds later she was in, naked as Dominic, shocking him with her nakedness and appearance. Her legs were covered in a constellation of horseshoe-shaped bruises, coloured black and blue. They were frightening to look at, but he couldn't take his eyes from them.

'See enough?' she asked, her face angry and ready for battle.

He quickly looked away, embarrassed.

She must have been at least four years older than him, but he hardly knew the difference. Physically, neither of them had much to boast about to the world.

Quickly, Dominic swam away once he realised it was a girl he had to deal with. If Tommy Shields or Red Nolan saw him playing with a girl they'd never let him live it down. It would be all over town.

But the more he tried to escape, the more she laughed, disappearing underwater only to reappear seconds later beside him, splashing him.

The girl kept looking at him, strangely, as if he were some strange creature she had captured in a net.

'Why don't ya go to your own side of the lake?' suggested Dominic, annoyed each time her grinning face appeared. 'I was here first – and stop the hell lookin' at me like that. Are you a freak or somethin'?'

His remark only enticed her to aggravate him further, and she proceeded to inform him that a snake was slowly moving towards him, its mouth wide open, fangs at the ready.

Dominic knew she was lying, yet he turned in panic to see.

'Chicken,' she shouted. 'Snakes just love chicken!'

He had had enough, and attempted to swim to the edge, escape the bug-head girl, get dried and make his way home.

But she was having none of that.

'You'll go when I let you go, Chicken Boy,' she said, holding his arm tightly. Her strength was deceiving, for a girl, and she squeezed tighter, watching if he would flinch.

Dominic didn't want to hit her, he was above that sort of thing, but his patience was running out.

'What's your name, Chicken Boy?' She was staring straight into his eyes, burrowing deep with an intensity that made Dominic blink.

'None of your business. Anyway, you smell,' he replied, hoping to sting her.

It failed and she simply laughed. 'If that's the best you can do, Chicken Boy, I'm gonna let you go, but not before you cry. Show me some tears.'

She dug her fingernails deep into his skin, never taking her eyes from his face, watching his eyes, waiting.

The pain was unbearable. Her nails felt like hot needles. He knew his skin was pierced, knew he was bleeding, but he would not give in. The water on his waist became colder and his teeth began to rattle so loud he hated himself.

His stubbornness fuelled her further as she dug the nails down deeper. '*Cry,*' she hissed through clenched teeth. '*Cry, Chicken Boy. Cry and I'll let you fly.*'

He couldn't help it, tried to prevent them, but slowly they came, running down his face, burning his skin.

She laughed, pushing him away, as if contaminated. 'Go, Chicken Boy. Fly back to your ma and da. Now! Before I really hurt you. Scat!'

A second later, she disappeared underwater, and he watched as ripples of her skin merged perfectly with the deepness of the lake blending her almost invisible. When she reappeared, she was a good ten feet away from him, grinning a sadistic grin.

Dominic was seething. He wished he could hurt her, as she had hurt him. Then, as if Joey Maxwell had whispered something in his ear, some terrible dark secret, it dawned on him who she was. Her mother owned the local rag store on the edge of town. The whole town spoke of her mother with such disdain and fear it was as if she were a witch. He knew, also, about the innuendos of dark whispers with their torn curtain of resentment, and suddenly he had the ammo he needed.

He waited until he was a good distance from her before letting her have it, both barrels blazing. 'Your ma's the town whore!' he screamed. 'The whole town has seen her hairy hole!'

The girl disappeared for what seemed an impossible time and for a heart-stopping second he thought the snakes had captured her. He didn't hate her that much and panic rose in his stomach.

Without warning, she was on his back, pushing him under with all her weight, making him swallow great gulps of the stinking water and muck.

She held him down and he watched as his hands moved in slow motion. Her grip was relentless, and he realised in his fear and struggling that she was trying to kill him. No one would know. The snakes would eat his corpse and the town would call him a dead fool, swimming after being told not to.

It was perfect.

Dominic felt the water flood his brain and suddenly Joey Maxwell appeared, swimming towards him, laughing. Behind him swam Dominic's great aunt Kathy, dead five years.

Aunt Kathy had never liked Dominic and he knew she was going to give him a piece of her mind, but just as she opened her mouth, he found himself on the bank, staring at the terrifying face of the girl. There was a smile on her face, but not a smile associated with humans. It was almost animal-like in its fierceness.

He wanted to scream at her, for trying to murder him, but all he could do was cough out bits of mud and water. Tears were in his eyes with fright and pain. He didn't care who saw them. His pride, like Joey, was dead.

'You even cry like a little chicken,' she sneered, dressing quickly. 'The next time, I'll not be so merciful.' She stood to go, but not before giving his ribs and face a nice kick. 'That'll help you throw up the rest, maybe a frog, if you're lucky.' Then, as if having second thoughts, she bent down and whispered in his battered face, her voice a menacing hiss. 'Don't *ever* speak about my ma like that again. You do, I'll kill you.' She sank her teeth into his lips, sending a beam of pain through him, making him cry again.

Seconds later she was gone, and he wondered if it had all been a crazy dream. Only the pain in his ribs and the blood trickling down his chin told the truth.

Three hours later he was in hospital, his lips needing six stitches, the pain indescribable. He would never forget that pain, he vowed to himself as he walked home, distraught and battered. More importantly, he would never forget the one who caused it.

Chapter Six

Saturdays. Dominic loved Saturdays. A lie in bed; perhaps a matinee over at "The Donkey" movie house to see Bond or Count Dracula, and later *Bonanza* on the telly. But most of all, he loved Saturdays because his father would arrive home from the boats, money in his pockets.

Sometimes – not always – Dominic saw some of the money go into his pocket accompanied by that wink that said not to be telling his mother. Dominic loved that secret because he was getting one over on her. Timmy received nothing.

Once, last year, Timmy had blabbered it all over the house that he had money hidden in his room, just like the pirates.

There was murder that night, as his mother accused his father of hoarding his wages.

'How the hell am I supposed to run this establishment if you go handing out your wages – my money – to every Tom, Dick, Timmy and Dominic? Don't you earn little enough without pretending to be a millionaire? Or maybe I'm mistaken. Have you become the captain, without me knowing? Is that it? Has a miracle happened?'

Dominic hated the way his father would not defend himself, sitting there like a sheep to be slaughtered.

'It's only a pittance, Julia. To get themselves some sweets, for God's sake,' his father replied, that ridiculous grin on his face.

'A pittance? Is that what you call it? That's what you hand me each week. A damn pittance. If it weren't for my lodgers, we'd all be out in the street. And don't you ever forget that, John Tranor. And don't dare curse at me again.'

It was a long time after that before Dominic received some pocket money. 'What ever you do, son, don't let your mother find it. We'll all be dead. And for heaven's sake, don't let Long Timmy Silver find it. He'll have us all walkin' the plank.'

Yes, Saturdays could be good, except when he saw that "smile" on his mother's face. That "smile" meant only one thing.

'As soon as you've finished your breakfast, there are apples in the yard, ready for Mister Fleming,' she said, handing him a slice of toast.

No. I refuse to go there. I hate it. You can't make me do something I hate. I'm not gonna do it. I'm not my da.

But, like his father, these were only dream words, words that probably would never come from his mouth.

His appetite gone, Dominic made a move for the door.

'Don't forget the apples,' said his mother, indicating with her thumb a large box in the corner.

It was raining outside, but with a hushed quietness associated usually with snow. Dominic watched intently, picturing the rain's needles of porcupine quills bouncing in slow motion and forming puddles the size and colour of burnt pennies. It looked as if it would rain all day so he decided to make a move towards Fleming's, the greengrocer. Better to get it over with. Hopefully, no one in the street would see him carrying the battered box of apples towards the shop.

Approaching the greengrocer's, Dominic stopped to watch the horses utilised by the local glazier. They stood in unison, eating, pissing and shitting. They never stopped, their arses perpetually pushing out fist-size boulders with slivers of undigested straw protruding from them like burnt cacti. Kamikaze sparrows darted in and out between the horses' legs capturing the spillage of oats and grain.

Sometimes his mother made him scoop up the dung to fertilise the trees, much to the amusement of the kids in the street. He had wanted to poison the horses, burn down the trees, make his mother eat her precious dung, and even though these were only thoughts, they became at times so tangible he could taste them.

Resigned to his fate, Dominic took a deep breath before entering the shop, before having to deal with Fleming, the Dog from Hell.

The shop itself was a mongrel, a puzzlement of newspapers, raw fish and fruit. Great slabs of meat, sprinkled with sweaty salt, were perched along the back wall, exposed on unforgiving "S" hooks. The carcasses resembled a grotesque, Bosch-like madness of ruddy violin-shaped sheep and cello cows.

There were flies everywhere, buzzing and humming, banging off the large store window. Dead flies lined the window like a military convoy debilitated by superior forces, while their airborne comrades struggled above on dirty, sticky paper

Dominic stared at the adhesive, fascinated by its struggling victims trying in vain to detach themselves from the sticky graveyard. It always reminded him of the currant buns sold next door in *Mullan's Bakery*. He had never tasted one in his life. Never would.

Yet, despite all this, the store always had an exotic feel; when passing through the doors from the street, you felt as if you had entered some strange, alien world, foreign and cluttered, as if its untold stories would fill a universal library, filling it to the brim with darkness and mystery.

The shop's floor lay in an uneven wave, de-crucified by time and wear and covered in thick sawdust. When walked upon, it released the rustic scent of pine into the air.

'Ah! Young Dominic!' exclaimed Fleming, attired in a blood-spattered apron, crowbar in hand. 'Good to see you're not like the rest of the dirty dogs, sleeping in their beds on a beautiful mornin' like this.' It was still pouring outside.

Fleming squeezed the teeth of the crowbar between the lips of a banana crate and with a slight movement of his elbow, popped the wood asunder.

'How many, young Dominic?' asked Fleming, a giant with tight pants and a filthy tight waistcoat. The man's large stomach had sheltered too many beers for its own good.

'50, Mister Fleming,' squeaked Dominic. He hated this part, the barter of apples.

Fleming handled one of the apples, rubbing his thumb against the texture, smelling it with his giant nostrils.

'Four cabbages. Howsabouthathen?' He said this as one word.

'My mother said *five* cabbages, four carrots and a stone of blue spuds.'

Dominic wished Fleming would hurry, fearing that one of the neighbours might come in, witnessing this humiliating act.

'Ha! Your mother's arse is out the window,' laughed Fleming, who was now juggling some of the apples, like a clown, into the air, winking as he pretended to allow them to fall. 'But you've caught me in a generous mood. Four cabbages – and here's some carrots as well.'

Dominic was not in the mood, so he didn't argue. Besides, in the end, Fleming would win. He always did.

'Don't forget this,' said Fleming, handing a ruffled bag to Dominic.

Reluctantly, Dominic accepted the unwanted 'gift'. He knew its contents and detested it; detested the power it had over his mother, the Jekyll and Hyde capabilities it processed.

Fleming smiled then winked at Dominic's hesitancy. 'Don't you worry, lad. Your mother's wee secret is safe with me. That's damn good brandy. Don't forget to tell her that.' The words were slippery, like a snail captured by the sun. Dominic would remember Fleming's words years after the greengrocer was dead.

As Dominic prepared to leave the shop, Fleming shoved a pear into his hand. The fruit was badly bruised and had teeth marks in it. 'Here, that's for you. And tell your mother she's gotta get up early to catch me!'

Dominic could still hear the laughter halfway down the lane and he knew his mother would look on the exchange with disdain.

'That's all?' she asked as he entered the kitchen.

'*Why didn't you go yourself?*'

His mother was shocked. 'How dare you speak to me like that!' she screamed, slapping him hard on the face, opening up the wounded lip as she brought her hand up again to strike.

He didn't flinch, despite the pain. He hadn't forgiven himself for crying at the lake and vowed never to cry again – for anything, anyone.

When his mother froze, Dominic thought it was embarrassment, but he quickly realised she was confused. Normally, he would have covered his face from further blows, but he simply stared into her eyes, the way that strange girl had looked into his.

'Don't look at me like that,' she said, threateningly. 'Don't dare look at me like that again.' She brought her hand down. 'Now, get the shovel. Fill that bucket. That'll give you something to think about. All the so-called men in this house are useless. If it weren't for me, none of you would ever know what to do. Now get out of my sight!'

Dominic lifted the bucket and headed for the street, and even though the other kids would laugh as he shovelled the shit, deep down he felt good. Something had changed in him, something forever. He couldn't describe it, but he knew it had happened.

No, he decided, *there'll be no more shovelling shit for Dominic Tranor.* Triumphantly, he tossed the bucket down the street, now caring who it hit, what it smashed, then quickly climbed the drainpipes that reached all the way to the top of the school.

As he reached the top, the caretaker screamed from a window that he was going to call the cops. But Dominic ignored the threats. He knew the man was bluffing. How could heavy cops master the fragile and rusty drainpipe that sighed wearily under his youthful weight?

As he sat there, invisible to all except those empowered with flight, his mind began to fill with the imagery of velvet butterflies and cooing, fat-bellied pigeons.

From the roof, he could hear the whisper of distant traffic. A handball game was in progress down below, and he could discern bare hands slapping, slicing and aiming for points as the ball made hypnotic, heartbeat thumps. Hope and triumph manifested themselves in the voices of the untiring players. Gazing towards the yards at the back of the houses, he could see the washing lines full of fluttering clothes resembling gulls scampering for food, while dirty water snaked through the arteries in the pavement, suffusing with discarded oil from an abandoned car that lay like a great wounded beast against the scrap-yard wall.

'Come here often?' asked a voice, breaking his thoughts.

Dominic turned to see the smiling face of Larkin.

'What do you want?' asked Dominic, wondering how the hell Larkin had managed to climb the drain without making a sound. 'Can't you find someone to play with? Now take yourself back down. You don't belong up here. This is my wee spot.'

Larkin continued smiling. 'I didn't know you owned the school, Mister Tranor. Anyway, I've brought you something.'

'If it's a foot, stick it up your arse.'

'Here. Take it,' he said, holding out an envelope.

'What is it?' Dominic rose to his feet.

'You'll never know if you don't open it.'

Dominic tore the envelope open and was shocked by its monetary content.

'Where did you get this?'

'Nosey.' Larkin touched the tip of his nose. 'Just stick it in your pocket, and don't let your ma or da find it.'

The envelope was the same as the type used for the Sunday collection at Saint Peter's. A look of horror crossed Dominic's face.

'You didn't steal this from the church, did you? From the Poor Clare's basket?'

Larkin laughed. 'Don't be silly. I keep all my money in those things. It stops my ma from asking too many questions. If she comes across it, I tell her I'm collectin' for the poor black babies. Anyway, those so-called Poor Clares are anythin' but poor. The Rip-Off Clares, I call them. It's my ma's money, from the shop. It was my da's shop, but when he died he left it to my ma. I'm entitled to some of it, don't you think?' Larkin pulled out a cigarette, lit it up before extending the box to Dominic.

'No. I hate those things, their smell and what they do to people. I saw a programme on the –'

'Fuck sake, you're almost fourteen. You're not a kid anymore, Dominic. You've gotta start growin' up.' Larkin blew smoke down his nostrils like an exhausted dragon. 'Anyway, who gave you that face and lip? I'd bet it was Nutter.'

Dominic's lip was still wet from the new bleeding and his face still carried the forget-me-not bruises. He had no taste for the conversation's direction. 'You'd lose. It wasn't that scumbag. Just drop it.'

'I can fix that bastard for you. Really. Was it him?'

Dominic wanted to laugh at the thought of Larkin "fixin'" Nutter, but his mouth was too sore.

'You're worse than my ma, except she hardly mentioned it. Said it served me right, that I must have done somethin' to deserve it.'

'Did you?'

'What?'

'Deserve it?'

For the first time this morning, Dominic smiled. 'I think I did.'

They both laughed.

Larkin turned to leave.

'You don't have to go. Stay up here. It's a great view.'

'I can't. Not at the minute. We've a delivery of meat coming today and I've got to be in the shop. My mother isn't feelin' too . . .' Larkin's voice trailed off.

Dominic quickly seized the moment of awkward silence. 'Look . . . before you go, I want to say . . . you know, for that stupid remark about your ma. My own ma's nothin' to boast about. Seems I've been makin' fun of everyone's ma, lately.'

'Forget it.' Larkin reached and touched Dominic's shoulder. 'I have power, Dominic, power that can be yours for the asking. If only you believe. Power that can turn even Nutter into dust and mangled bones.'

Dominic smiled awkwardly, dreading any talk of Nutter. As far as Dominic was concerned, Nutter had the ability to hear every single bad word whispered about him.

'No thanks,' replied Dominic. 'I like Nutter just the way he is.'

Larkin said nothing, as he disappeared back down the side of the roof.

Opening the envelope again, Dominic counted at least three weeks of pocket money.

'Three weeks of pocket money,' he told himself, over and over again as he made his way back down from the roof. What had started as a disaster that morning had somersaulted right back in his favour. Even the salty taste of blood in his mouth couldn't dampen his spirits as he debated with himself who would get the money. It would be a tossup between Sean Connery and Christopher Lee, with John Wayne as a possible runner-up. Only one thing was definite: it certainly wouldn't be going to squealer Timmy, and most definitely not his mother.

Chapter Seven

June slowly killed itself and July arrived with the same promise of boredom and mundane routines. Then came a day that changed Dominic's life forever, a day filled with rushing daylights that banished the misery of a squeaky voice and spotted skin.

He left home early for Jackson Lake, but not before making a sandwich of bread and jam and popping his latest Perry Mason paperback into his bag.

A good 30 minutes later he arrived near his spot at the lake, just as the sun was skimming along the water, reflecting it like a giant mirror. The air was cool, but he knew by the time he stepped into the water it would be warm. All the weathermen predicted it. If he got a quick dip before someone else came, he could enjoy a couple of chapters along with his sandwich. He wasn't going to allow anyone to stop him using the lake – least of all some smelly girl who thought she was a boy.

Stripping, he wasted no time before plunging straight in. The water was surprisingly cold, but he loved it. Being naked added something forbidden to it. His mother would snap if she knew this was how he swam. The thought made him smile as he emerged from the water before quickly drying himself.

It was usually about this time of year when Dominic felt frustrated by the false hype surrounding the summer break. It was as false as the dreams he had of becoming a journalist or a lawyer. He knew he would probably end up working in Stark Timber Yard or the abattoir over at Tower Street. Everyone ended up there. He would be no exception.

'At least there'd be meat on the table,' he whispered bitterly. 'Keep her happy.'

He thought about the bread and book and couldn't decide which would be enjoyed the most. Hunger told him the bread; curiosity told him the third chapter of the book, the chapter where Perry starts to smell a rat.

'The bread can wait. Perry can't; not while justice needs to be done.'

Dominic had watched every episode of Perry Mason, could recite, verbatim, each line he spoke, especially his closing speech when you just knew he was going to mesmerize the jury with his command of language and logic.

This was Dominic's dream: saving the unjustly accused, catching the killer, tidying up all the loose ends. Newspapers would write about him; perhaps interviews on national television and radio. Anything was possible, with dreams.

The day had started unusually wet for July, and the ground was still moist despite the heat, releasing tiny fingers of steam into the air. He placed his damp towel on the ground and opened up the book, and within seconds was absorbed into the fascinating conflict between crime, punishment and justice.

'What's ya readin', Chicken Boy?'

He hadn't heard her creep up on him and the sound of her voice ringed his stomach with ice. He winced involuntarily. Remnants of the stitches still hung ghoulishly from his lower lip, and suddenly the pain returned to it, throbbing uncontrollably.

Tight, against her scruffy jeans, she held an evil-looking

knife, its serrated teeth grinning wickedly, the blade an extension of herself. Blood was still reflecting on it, wet and terrifying.

He wondered where the blood came from and what she was going to do; wondered if he would pee his pants – maybe worse.

'Not gonna tell me?' She dropped something down beside him, something so heavy it made a dull thud, forcing him to look. Hares, four or five of them bundled together, dead, their massive paws tied with old cord.

Uninvited, she knelt down beside him.

'Perry Mason. He's a lawyer,' Dominic managed to squeak, his voice rusted with fear.

He wondered if anyone had spotted her coming? Was this part of her plan, to finish him here, no witnesses? The throbbing in his lips became more acute.

'A *law* book? Are you plannin' to be a lawyer, Chicken Boy? Save all the good people in town, burn the bad?'

He resented being called Chicken Boy and felt a tiny bubble of anger threatening to surface. But he struggled to contain it, knowing she was capable of something he wouldn't like.

'Cat got your tongue? Or maybe just your lip?' She brought the knife to his face and calmly placed it on the tip of his nose. The smell of animal blood filled his nostrils but he willed himself not to allow the beads of sweat that had formed in his scalp to trickle down, giving her the satisfaction of seeing how frightened he was.

He wondered what was coming – when it was coming.

As if reading his mind, she brought the knife down to the wounded lip, and in a flash cut the dangling threads with all the precision of a surgeon.

'Loose ends could get a person killed. Don't you know that?' She smiled at her own wit, and then shocked him by apologising, sort of. 'Back there, in the lake, didn't need to have happened. You shouldn't have said what you said.'

She was right, 110 per cent, so he did the right thing and apologised right back, sort of.

'You didn't need to have done what you done,' he replied, his voice oiled by her almost contrite response.

'Friends?' She put out her hand.

Dominic couldn't help notice the patchy spots of blood on the hand. Reluctantly, he shook it. 'Friends.'

She was looking at him, once again with that strange force in her eyes. He tried looking away, but failed. 'I never see you with any of the other town kids. Guess you're too good for them now that you're gonna be a lawyer?'

'All of my friends go to Archangel, over at Staton. I only have one or two real friends from town,' he replied, defensively, hating his voice for its apologetic whine.

'*Real* friends? No such thing as *real* friends. Anyway, you've one less. That idiot, Joey Maxwell.'

It was a cruel remark, but he found himself smiling, and then laughing, probably with nerves.

'Ever been sketched?' she asked, breaking his gaze that strangely seemed to have made her uncomfortable, reversing the roles as she removed a rucksack from her back.

He wasn't too sure what she meant. 'No. I don't think so.'

From the rucksack she removed a pad and some pencils, placing them on the ground, next to him. He could see rough sketches of trees and wildlife and couldn't help noticing the family of hares, posing happily for the artist as they nibbled on grass. There was no doubt in his mind that the bodies a few feet away were one and the same crew. He found that morbid and once again she read his mind.

'Sketched them yesterday, prior to setting my traps. As I sketched them, I told them I was goin' to immortalize them. Do you know what that big word means, Chicken Boy?'

'Don't call me that. Okay?'

'Well, if I knew your name, I could use that instead. Couldn't I?'

'Dominic,' he replied. 'What's yours?'

'Don't be smart. Everyone knows my name is Dakota.'

He thought about getting up, leaving this strange, offensive girl and her dead bodies. But he couldn't move – didn't want to move. Something held him and he didn't resist.

'I'm gonna sketch you, so don't even think of blinkin'. You move – you're dead,' she said, smiling a dry and unconvincing smile as she wet the tip of a pencil with her tongue, leaving it the colour of liquorice.

For the next few minutes, all that could be heard was the sandy scratch of pencil on rough paper.

As she studied him, he studied her, her movement of fingers, her frown as she couldn't quite capture the intended likeness. But mostly he studied her face. Tiny fading freckles like rusted nail heads congregated under her eyes, giving them an almost dreamy-like look. Her upper lip slanted strangely, like a snarl, yet seductive. She reminded him of a young Lauren Bacall.

'Do you sketch everythin' before you kill it?' he whispered jokingly through clenched teeth, speaking like a ventriloquist's dummy.

For a second he saw the anger return to her eyes. 'I sketched my ma two years ago. She's still alive. More than you'll be if you open your mouth again.'

Finally, it was over and she began to pack. Although the day had been warm, it was nearly evening now, and the temperature had dipped dramatically.

'When do I get to see my picture?' He could imagine the way he was going to appear: a donkey, ears overlapping or, more likely, a chicken with a book under its wing.

'*Your* picture? Who said *you* owned it? If you're lucky you might see it soon; you might see it later,' she replied. 'Perhaps you mightn't see it at all. Ever . . .' Without warning, she quickly turned her face and kissed him hard, causing their teeth to clink like early-morning milk bottles. It was an awkward, nervous kiss, but it was his first real kiss and he felt it burn his stitched lips, as he tasted her breath. Blood heated his face with embarrassment.

She giggled. 'Why the reddner? Haven't you been with a girl before?' A strange look of puzzlement appeared on her face as she tilted her head, resting it on her shoulders.

'Of course I have,' replied Dominic, defensively. 'Lots.'

She smiled and reached out her hand. 'C'mon. Over here,' she said, guiding him to the old green hut that functioned as toilet, shelter and storage. Its hoary paint was peeling, revealing initials of lovers long gone.

Without warning, she opened her shirt and placed his hand on her breast. It was warm and small, like an egg after a hen goes to feed. He could feel her heart beat, pulsating through the skin.

She leaned to him and he could smell *Lifebouy* soap and *Sunsilk* shampoo oozing from her.

'Do you like me, Dominic?' she whispered.

His head was spinning. He never knew things like this existed. Oh yes, it was always the topic at school, talked about on numerous occasions by pretenders and frustrated virgins, but to actually experience the unimaginable, to be here, right at this moment, was tantamount to touching something he never truly believed existed.

'Say, I like you,' she asked softly, her voice no longer harsh and cynical.

'I like you,' he managed to say, his throat sandpaper-dry with anticipation, her smells intoxicating him, filling him with strange power he never knew he possessed. He could hear things that were impossible: the mist settling on the lake; stones breathing in the baking heat. He could even taste the sun in his mouth as they kissed, big wet kisses that seemed to last an eternity, glistening their mouths with eagerness. Even the throbbing pain in his lips was gone, replaced with something more powerful, something perfect that could never be created again.

Between them they had served less than 30 years on earth, but this moment in time filled him with the youthful hallucinations of immortality, of deities in miniature.

It was at that precise moment, he fell in love.

'One day, when I think you're ready, I'll let you go further than just touching my breasts. But things like that have to be earned. Do you understand, Dominic?'

Further? What was she talking about? He couldn't believe he had actually touched her breasts, squeezed the hardness of her nipples, which reminded him of gobstoppers sucked down to their last level. He could still feel the dry talc feeling of her breasts on his hands, warming them as fear crept in. Would his mother be able to smell that strange smell? Would she know what he had just done?

'You haven't answered me, Dominic. Do you understand what I just said?'

Dakota's words broke the trance.

'Yes . . . I understand . . .'

To complete a perfect day, she produced an orange from her rucksack, nipped its skin and tunnelled under it with her fingers, releasing pellets of citrus into the air.

He would remember that smell forever as she tore the orange in half and shared.

Contented, Dominic lay back on the grass and began to hum.

'Don't,' she said.

He stopped. 'What? Don't what?'

'Hum. I hate it.'

She had her back to him as she spoke, but her voice had an edge to it so he let the subject drop.

He cursed himself for annoying her, but when she turned and faced him, touching his hair, he knew he was forgiven.

'One day I'll be an artist,' she said, as the sun warmed their faces. 'World famous.' She laughed and laughed, squeezing her eyes tight with joy.

He laughed with her until she stopped abruptly, whispering, 'I'll paint my pain with his blood. Paint the sky with it.'

Her words touched his spine, making him shiver. Tiny stones moved in his stomach. He reached out to touch her but his fingers felt wrong. They were numb.

'Whose blood, Dakota?' What the hell had she meant by that?

'Someone . . . someone I know. Someone you know.'

The sweaty proximity of fear touched him for a second, making his skin tighten, then was gone. Had he been wiser, perhaps the corollary of her words would have had meaning and the summer's sweetness might not have tasted so wickedly good. But the words meant nothing. Instead, it was the summer of his life, etched forever, changing him utterly.

'Tell me,' he persisted. 'What's his name?'

'Do you know the strength of love, what it can do?' she asked, looking at his profile, touching it with a blade of grass.

The question confused him, so he simply smiled hoping she wouldn't ask again.

'Love can kill, without question, without doubt. It can free a prisoner faster than a key. Do you think you could love me, Dominic?'

There was only one answer in his head. 'Yes. I'll always love you, Dakota.'

'Always?'

'Always.'

He smiled to himself, closing his eyes with pleasure, never seeing the dead look on her face, sheltered in secrets and shadows.

Suddenly, as if bitten by an insect, Dominic sprang to life, tilting his head towards the overgrowth. 'Did you hear somethin'? Over there, near the bushes?'

They both became still, listening intently, but all that could be heard was the lake skimming in silence, touching rocks with its soft groans, like a hiss made by a nail in a tire.

'No,' she replied. 'You're just nervous.'

Somewhere in the woods they could hear a cuckoo. The bird moved heavily, causing leaves to filter down on top of them, while all the time she stared at him with that same intense gaze she had had in the lake. 'A bird. Told you it was nothin',' she said, pushing herself up, wiping off the blades of grass and leaves. 'It's gettin' late. We should be goin'.'

The sun began to slowly spill into the earth, bringing the beginning of tomorrow's cool wind bleeding northwards.

Dominic liked to listen to the wind while he waited for the school bus in the mornings, but this wind made the hair on the back of his head feel funny.

When the sun finally died, the sky was still light from where it shone somewhere else, leaving fingers of silver and red across the sky.

But not in the park, where darkness came quickly and the clouds looked threatening as they released tiny drops of rain.

The streets became deserted as Dakota and Dominic made their way along Gracemore Street, the industrial part of town. Suddenly, the drizzle became heavy. Runnels of rain snaked their way through the tangle of arteries in the pavements of the street while overhead, thunder boomed.

'Run!' shouted Dominic. 'We'll be soaked!'

But Dakota held him tight, a prisoner against the gable wall of Gracie's Cold Storage Factory and they kissed, big, opened-mouth kisses, while the rain ran off their skin and into their mouths, allowing them to taste each other's saltiness.

Eagerly, she gripped his hair tight and kissed his chin, his cheeks, his eyes, then his wounded lips, sucking them so tightly he felt pain reaching down his spine.

Oh what a beautiful pain.

Without warning, Dominic pushed Dakota to the side, as if he had been contaminated. 'How long have you been standin' there, watchin'?' he asked.

Larkin stood two feet away, a cigarette dangling from his mouth.

'Long enough. Who's this?' he asked, using the lit cigarette as a pointer, aiming it directly into Dakota's face.

Outraged, Dakota slapped it from his hand and closed in on him. 'Don't ever point at me again – especially with a lit cigarette. Do you understand?'

The hairs on Dominic's neck tingled. There was something in her tone that just made him want to die.

Quickly, he ended the inevitable confrontation. 'Dakota. Her name's Dakota. Satisfied?'

Larkin and Dakota glared at each other, a bewildered Dominic trapped between them. He wondered if Dakota would make a comment about Larkin's scars, hurt him with her scorpion tongue, but quickly realised that it would have little effect. Larkin's eyes probably told her that he had armoured himself against all verbal abuse.

'Want to go to *Gino's*, Dominic?' asked Larkin, refusing to take his eyes from Dakota. 'A fish supper would hit the spot, don't you think?'

Dominic bit down on his lip. He could taste the fish in his mouth being washed down with *Coke*. 'I can't,' he finally mumbled.

Larkin smiled. 'You're sure? Okay then, I'll see you about – both of you.'

They both waited until he was out of sight.

'I bet it was him at the lake, watchin' us,' said Dominic, breaking the silence.

'I don't like him,' replied Dakota.

'He is a bit weird, but once you get to know him, he's okay.'

'Where did he get those scars? He looks like Frankenstein.'

'Don't, Dakota. Don't make fun of his face,' replied Dominic, defensively. 'Everyone makes fun of him.'

'Oh, did I touch a nerve, Dominic? Is there somethin' you're not tellin' me? Do you and Larkin touch each other in places not allowed? Is that why you've never been with a girl?'

Dominic's face reddened. She was back, the other Dakota, the hateful, heartless one.

'C'mon. I'll walk you home,' he said, not wanting to listen to the tongue.

'No. I can make my own way,' she replied, snapping at him, brushing him off like an annoying insect.

He watched her walk down the street, disappearing from view.

'Fine. I don't need you,' he whispered. 'Don't need you, ever.'

Chapter Eight

The other lodger in the house was a southern man by the name of John Costa. How long he had been staying at the house was impossible to say. Dominic could always remember Costa in the house, but someone in town had told him he had been there for five years, perhaps less.

Costa didn't talk much – at least to Dominic – and had a tiny ritual, which he performed each day without fail. After breakfast he would take his cane from the hallstand and not return until dinnertime – usually 1.00. Afterwards – weather permitting – he would sit in the garden for an hour, chain-smoking.

On his days off from school, Dominic would sit and watch Costa, the cocoon of smoke oozing from his face like an old gangster movie. The watching usually lasted about two minutes until his mother captured him, pulling his ear, hard. 'Stop spying on the man,' she would hiss with the threatening menace only his mother could conjure up. 'Get out and get the bloody air about you! Nosey, nosey, nosey!'

Initially, Dominic believed his mother was overly protective of Costa. Perhaps because he came from down south, or maybe as his friends would say, needling him: 'She fancies that big redneck, your ma. Gonna be your new da! Your old da's gettin' kicked out!'

It was nonsense, of course, thinking Costa would ever be his father. He knew his mother and father rarely spoke, but he was certain they still had feelings for each other, even if his father was only home one day of the week.

Finally, he decided that the reason for his mother's concern was that Costa had a leg missing, though to be honest no one would ever have guessed from the way he walked, his enormous back stiff as a board when he strolled down the street accompanied by his cane, his false, plastic leg stiff yet workable.

Costa's origins had been discussed more than the local greyhound results, but the missing leg had been a topic on its own. They spoke about it in *Datlow's* bar for ages until Tom Maguire, the local headmaster, told them all to shut their lousy mouths. 'The man lost his leg in Vietnam, where the dead outnumbered the living, a hell-on-earth place where none of you spineless bastards would last ten seconds.'

From that day, John Costa became a sort of celebrity in town. It was a pleasure to buy him a drink, if you were fortunate enough to meet him in the bar. Occasionally for his listeners, he would reveal a tiny fraction of the horror and madness of war, describing in detail the struggle for survival in a foreign land that hated you as much as you hated it. Yet, despite the row of medals sitting in his drawer, he was modest, almost shy when speaking of them.

"They're nothing. Really. They can't feed you when you're hungry" he would say with self-deprecating honesty that humbled his listener.

Of course, Dominic's mother didn't need to be told about the new *hero*. She had known it from the day he entered the house, soaked to the skin, barely talking. It was she who found the medals tucked away in an old suitcase, one morning as she cleaned out the room. For a woman who had loved John Wayne and every movie he had ever made, this was a godsend. The Quiet Man had returned, and even though she knew she was no Maureen O'Hara, she did have red hair.

It *was* nonsense, thinking Costa would ever replace his father, but that was before the incident that made Dominic realise that sometimes nonsense and reality can be the closest of neighbours . . .

That night of the incident, Dominic swore he had heard his mother's door open with a tiny accusing squeak, but when he glanced in the dark hallway from his room, nothing was there.

He tried to erase that moment in time from his brain, yet something was burning in him, distorting any logic that told him to stop being so childish, so stupid as to believe she would do anything so disgusting, so scandalous. But two nights later, with rain coming down like pearls, a sound floated to him. He had heard it before, but it was foreign. Tonight, however, it was fluent. He believed he knew its meaning now and it terrified him.

Quickly, he climbed out of bed and tiptoed up the stairs, up to where he didn't want to go.

Outside his mother's door, he listened to the blue silence as it knotted his stomach. He could hear her voice. Hollow, far away, as if descending from a well. He could hear soft laughter, whispered words and movements from her bed mingling with sheets touching skin.

Dominic wanted to tap on the door, hoping no one would answer, clearing his conscience with the provoked rational of a coward trapped in his own paralyses. Instead, he quickly slithered back to bed, relieved the door hadn't opened, cursing the whispers that had recruited his emotions, staining them with guilt.

Later that same week, he tried to find the courage to ask his mother to forgive him, for thinking such terrible thoughts. She was above the type of thing that had turned his brain septic. He wouldn't tell her exactly what his thoughts had been – it would be too embarrassing – but from here on in, he would become a better son, no more complaining, perhaps even find a wee job, bring some money to the house. She would like that.

It was quite by accident when he knocked the bin over in the yard, spilling its contents out on the ground, revealing the disgusting condom stuck to the bin lid, ballooned thickly with imagination and lust.

He had seen condoms before, in the park, where lovers went to do their thing. They always fascinated his young mind, but now, thinking that his mother would use them, filled him with revulsion and embarrassment.

Terrible scenes ripped into his head, scenes of his mother and the redneck, grunting like pigs, smelling of stale and forbidden sweat. He hated her – hated them both. Blood was boiling in his skull, telling him to expose her, make his father kill her and Costa.

Angrily, he stomped down on the horrible sheath, bursting its belly, splattering its creamy vomit all over the yard. '*Die!*' he screamed, not caring who heard.

'Have you gone crazy, down there?' shouted his mother, from the top window, preparing to clean it with a cloth. 'Get the hell inside the house before the neighbours see you. I don't know what to do with you . . . you're starting to do my head in.'

Dominic thought about shouting back at her, tell her every little detail in his head. But he didn't, because a painful understanding came to him, an understanding so grim he could only scream in his head, pounding it with his fists: exposing his her filthy secret would cause more devastation to his father than it would her.

But he vowed to himself that one day he *would* reveal it, shouting it from the rooftops for all to hear; expose her dirty tricks for all the neighbours to see. And he would relish that moment, like the mouth of a fox on the chicken's neck, crunching it in his teeth.

Chapter Nine

July was approaching its end when Dominic finally decided to get his act together by heading over to Lancaster Street Library to pick through what small amount of books it had in its collection.

He hadn't seen Dakota in weeks, not since Larkin spoiled everything. He could barely sleep without seeing her cruel face torturing him. Everyone – everything – ceased to exist. His books became irrelevant obstacles that prevented him from thinking about her. When he tried to think of Perry Mason he became Bogart instead, winking at her as she smiled back, her dark eyes promising him the unimaginable, something he had yet to taste.

A few hours later, he emerged from the building's dull interior to the bleaching sunlight of early noon, to be greeted by her voice. 'I thought you'd died in there. What kept you?'

He shouldn't have smiled like an idiot, showing her his weakness. But he was like a dog, waiting obediently for its master to return.

'If I'd known you were out –'

She cut him off, her hand held up like a traffic cop over at Swindon Avenue.

'C'mon.'

They walked what seemed for hours. There was little if any talk from her and Dominic obeyed her silence, fearful she would chastise him, sending him running for home. He noticed how people stared at them – at her – as they left the town's boundary. Their eyes should have been filled with jealousy, instead it was hate; hate for her but more so him, for allowing himself to be with her, to want her.

'Where are we goin'?' he finally asked, legs aching.

'We're here,' she smiled, nodding at an enormous church, its swelling shadow eating up half the street. They had crossed over into Syracuse Heights, an up-and-coming town that put their own to shame.

'This is where I get my inspiration for some of my work. The Church of the Misbegotten. C'mon.'

Dominic stepped inside, intimidated by the vastness and unfamiliar smells of candles and incense and statues of agonising angels with ordained, majestic faces. Their own church, Saint Peter on the Rock, was a hovel in comparison.

Misty lighting infused his imagination further, making the quietness eerily, like being trapped in a shadow's echo. Dakota tugged gently on his arm as she gave him a tour of the great place. 'These are reproductions of Old Masters. Aren't they incredible? See how their eyes follow you, as if they are watchin', silently stalkin'?'

Creepy, was the word Dominic wanted to use, but he said nothing. If she loved them, he loved them.

'He's my favourite,' she whispered, pointing at a painting attached to the wall. 'El Greco. His models came from the lunatic asylum in Toledo and the local prison. Did you know that?'

Of course he didn't. He had only heard of this El Whatever,

a minute ago. His ignorance made him angry and she saw it. He knew she was laughing at him, deliberately needling him with her superiority and intelligence.

'Think about it, Dominic. All those child molesters and rapists, murderers and perverts, transformed to saints on canvas. Powerful, isn't it, the way the eye can lie?'

He looked about the church, hoping no one could hear her. He wasn't religious, but he became defensive.

'You shouldn't talk like that, Dakota. Not in a church.'

'Like what? Truthful, you mean? Why?' She pointed at a large crucifix suspended in mid-air. 'Terrified He might come down from that cross and kick you in the balls? There's not a hope of that happenin', Dominic. Know why? Because He doesn't fuckin' exist. Even you should have figured that out by now.'

'*Dakota!*' he hissed. '*Don't curse in church.*'

She looked at him with that power to kill, the power that she alone possessed.

'Don't curse in church?' she replied, sarcastically. 'That's a rhyme. You should be a poet, except you can hardly write your name, can you? You think you're gonna be a lawyer, a somebody? Ha! You'll die in Monroe Town – just like me.'

'You might be right,' he said, calmly, putting into practice his lawyer voice. 'But that doesn't give you the right to be disrespectful in a church.'

She threw her head back, laughing so loud people glared in her direction.

An elderly women, her head shrouded in a shawl, glared at both of them. '*Ssshhh!*' demanded the woman.

'Ssshhh yourself, you old bitch!' challenged Dakota, as she moved towards the woman.

Fearful of what Dakota would do to the woman, Dominic pleaded as he held her arm, fearful of releasing it. 'Please, Dakota. I've seen enough. It was wonderful, but we can come back tomorrow, when the place isn't so full. I'd really love that.'

For a few terrible moments, he no longer existed, as Dakota stared at the older woman who seemed oblivious to the potential danger.

'Please, Dakota . . .'

'Let go of my arm,' she said quietly but firmly, her face slowly resuming normality. Then, as if nothing had happened, she said, 'C'mon. I'm gonna show you where I get the rest of my inspiration from, Mister Good Christian.' She grabbed his hand, making him run, their sounds thundering like hooves in the church.

Outside, the sun floated on a ghostly haze as they entered the narrow street with its gang of homeless people covered in liquid shadows, their slim belongings nipping at their feet. It was a part of the city he had never visited before, and, like most people, the monsters the mind creates without permission intimidated him.

One man, both legs amputated at the knee, was sitting in a dilapidated wheelchair. Older than his years, his face sagged, as if the dogs of poverty and depression had stolen every bone from it highlighting tiny dark webs which etched his eyes. The image made him think of Costa.

At one time these people were the salt of the earth, pillars of society. Now they were the dregs, witnessed but unseen, screaming apocalyptic profanities.

Near the end of the street, a bulging garbage bag lay gutted revealing a desiccated sanitary towel, which protruded from it like a bloody tongue panting in the heat. The stench oozing from the bag was stomach churning. Large flies clung like grapes, devouring the unthinkable, making the bag's stomach move with an invisible force.

As Dominic sidestepped the bag, a man covered in a ragged shroud bumped him, mumbling, 'Dirty my skin with bruises, punk? Ya betta kill me – cuz I'm cumin' fer ya! See? *See?* Whaddya hear, whaddya *sssayyy?*' His eyes were dead, like rotten knots on a diseased tree, his lips and tongue carpeted in baked-bean sauce and sores cemented with pus.

Dominic became frightened, but tried desperately not to show it. Dakota would ridicule him.

'These are *my* apostles,' she said, studying his reaction. 'And not a traitor among them.'

Slowly, Dominic backed off, as if they were closing in on him, ready to grab.

'Hug them, my wee duck,' she teased. 'Prove what a great Christian you are. Give them a big wet French kiss. Put your tongue on his sores. That's what your Hero on the cross would do. Prove me wrong, that you're not really a hypocrite like all the rest. Prove it . . .'

Her laughter was still in his ears as he ran home, hating her, hating himself.

Later, that same evening, Dominic heard Costa leave for the bar. They loved the big redneck down there, all those war stories for the price of a beer, scaring the shit out of them, allowing them to smell death and suffering, knowing they could all return to the safety of their little homes, afterwards.

Quickly he swallowed what remained on his plate before deciding to make his move. His mother was in the kitchen, and instead of heading towards the parlour, he did a sharp right turn and quietly crept up the stairs, stopping outside the lodgers' rooms.

He could hear Kane moving about, opening cupboards, humming to the radio's classical music playing softly in the background.

Slowly, he turned the handle of Costa's door before carefully edging it open.

Once inside, he quickly but gently closed the door, and listened to the sounds of the house. He couldn't prevent his heart from pumping in his ears, making hearing difficult as he admonished himself for this act of madness. His mother would kill him, but he found that thought as exciting as swimming naked. He smiled. *She's down there and I'm up here, right above her. I could shit on top of her and she wouldn't know what hit her.*

Tiptoeing carefully, he made his way across the floor, knowing she could hear a pin drop when it suited her. Unexpectedly, his eyes caught the gleam of plastic from the far corner of the room. A spare, false leg sat on the armchair. Dominic wanted to laugh. It made him think of the Invisible Man.

Gingerly he touched its mixture of wood and plastic, repulsed yet attracted to its horrible necessity. He could smell the faint aroma of ointment oozing from the hollowness as he brought the leg to his mouth, whispering and giggling, 'Is there anybody in there?' He thought about hiding it, breaking it somehow, but quickly realised this would be like squealing on himself.

'Oh, Larkin, you would love this. If you still had that rotten foot, you could stick it right down into the bottom of the false leg. Costa would never know – until it was too late. They would kick him out of the bar, him and his smelly leg. Wouldn't that be somethin'? Someone walkin' about with someone else's foot, not knowin'?'

Dominic stopped whispering. His ears had picked up a sound outside the door and suddenly his bravery was gone, as he heard the door handle turn.

He couldn't stop his heart banging; banging so loud it hurt his chest as the door slowly opened.

'John? Have you gone out, John?' whispered the secretive voice of Dominic's mother.

Dominic stopped breathing. If she turned the light on he would be exposed. He could see her perfectly, silhouetted in the door's frame, her massive head of hair starched like Medusa's.

'John?'

Could she see him, hear his heart, smell his fear? She was capable of that. This was worse than being captured by Nutter.

Slowly, she closed the door behind her, making not a sound, disappearing into the dark.

Was she in the room, or had she left? His mind raced. The dark became as silent and as immense as snow, torturing him with its nothingness. The blood in his head was seeping through his brain like ink on bread, causing confusion and panic. He couldn't think. He hadn't heard her footsteps go down the hall. Perhaps she was outside, waiting for him? Perhaps she was inside, waiting? That would be more like her.

To his relief, a minute later, Dominic heard the muffled sounds of his mother's and Kane's voices. Something about the evening being lovely.

Shaking, Dominic fell back in the chair, almost breaking the plastic leg. His own legs were trembling and his stomach had suddenly become empty. Cold sweat stuck to his forehead as he breathed in and out, slowly, but taking in great gulps of life-saving air, stillness came to his chest.

Perhaps he should have left, but he knew he had achieved nothing and was reluctant to go. His mother's unexpected appearance only galvanised his anger. He needed to find some sort of evidence. Anything. Find it. Expose her – them.

Feeling like Perry Mason's private investigator seeking evidence, Dominic searched the room for something incriminating to show his father when the time came, for future reference. The set of drawers looked inviting and he reached to open them.

Kane coughed, and Dominic's hand froze on the drawer's handle. His heart thumped louder, sending adrenaline coursing in his veins, exciting him further. Did he want to be caught? Was this what it was all about? Show his mother how insignificant she was? Let her know he knew? Perhaps.

He opened the drawer and searched, finding colourful silk neckties sitting, coiled up like beautiful snakes basking lazily in the sun. Next to them were underwear and socks. He wondered why a person with one leg needed pairs of socks. Wouldn't one be enough?

The bottom drawer surrendered nothing, only the hateful medals won with courage and distinction.

Reluctantly, Dominic touched the medals, wishing they belonged to his father. He would show them to every single person in school, in town – the world. They would all love his father, respect him, just like they did Costa, slapping him on the back, buying him drinks. His mother would love him, once again, just like she loved . . .

The large pouch was almost invisible, blending with the drawer's wood. He almost missed it. Almost.

Opening it, he pulled out the gathering of photographs. It was impossible to look at them in the dark so he turned on the tiny lamp near the bed, no longer caring about caution and consequences.

Nothing. Some of the pictures were so badly devastated with sepia he could barely make them out: grinning faces of skinny children at a beach; a woman smiling coyly, a basket of flowers in her hands. Three of the pictures showed Costa, younger, standing beside a house, an axe in his hand, shorts on. He looked weird. He had both his legs.

Before the war, Dominic supposed, hating the smile on Costa's movie-star face. 'Didn't know you'd be losin' your leg soon, did you?' he whispered, bitterly. 'Wonder how long after this picture was taken, did you lose the leg? A year? Two?'

Another picture was of Costa, surrounded by grinning friends, onboard what appeared to be a large ship. 'A war vessel,' whispered Dominic, hating himself for being in awe of it.

The pictures revealed nothing. They were as useless as the plastic leg laughing at him from the chair.

Angrily, he grabbed the leg and hit it against the wall, hard, not caring who could hear, not caring about the damage. He would smash the leg, and when Costa came through the door he would smash him, also.

A tiny package dropped at his feet, just as he took another swing at the wall.

Placing the leg back on the chair, he bent and picked the

package from the ground. It was wrapped in filthy plastic and secured by an elastic band.

It had been hidden inside the hollow of the leg, and like all good detectives Dominic understood that nothing ever hidden was mundane. Knowledge was power, but more powerful than power and knowledge combined is the discovered secret. Reasons and guilt – past, present and future – normally associated themselves with hidden objects, and he knew in his heart that this hidden treasure would be no exception and that sometimes – just sometimes – God truly did exist.

Quickly denuding the package, he set its contents on the table, his willing fingers carefully separating each photograph as his keen mind calculated their worth, their interpretation.

They were hazy images, yet a lot clearer than the ones in the drawer. Mainly they were of the boat, and for the first time Dominic could see the power of its size, its fearsome apparatus of war protruding from deck and spaces.

He didn't want to think of Costa on the boat. It made him think of his father down in the darkness of a ship's belly, cleaning out oil drums, the crew making jokes about how he looked like a monkey while they tossed rotten bananas at him. His father tried to make out it was funny, that was how things were on boats, but the seething anger in Dominic told him that Costa would never be covered in oil, and God help the man who would even think about throwing a banana in his direction – it would be the last time he'd ever throw a thing.

Dominic placed the picture on the tiny reading table. The pictures had revealed nothing. He knew there was a reason for their secrecy, but his mind refused to work out the puzzle. He felt a headache coming on. 'Dakota was right. I am dumb. Some lawyer I'd make . . .' It was the last group of pictures that began to talk, whispering, moving in his hand like a tiny movie. The great canons on the ship's deck were not canons. They resembled something from medieval times, like the giant catapult machines used to hurtle enormous boulders in an attempt to knock down castle walls.

The smudgy shadows – colossal in size – winked at him from the boat's deck, and suddenly his brain began to decipher their strange code of darkness, what they were, what they meant.

Whales, great tribes of them, hung from the boat's side, their great stomachs ripped and mangled beyond belief. It was a sickening sight, but still Dominic's eyes feasted on them, amazed by the slaughter of such gigantic creatures by such small opponents, grinning sadistically with their knives of steel.

Costa stood proudly on the head of one of the whales, smoking a cigarette, relaxing, not a care in the world. His entire body was covered in blood, giving him an eerie Halloween look, the look of a madman satisfied with his work.

The next couple of pictures told the same story. Nothing new – nothing revealed. But the last two pictures made Dominic stop. Costa was in bed. It looked like some makeshift hospital ward from an old war movie. A man stood by his side, his face grim. A doctor? A friend? The very last picture revealed a withered Costa ensconced in a wheelchair, smiling but subdued. A smile that said: so this is how it must end, a cripple, life destroyed?

'Dominic, Dominic, Dominic,' said the disapproving voice of John Costa who stood blocking the entire doorway with his massive frame. 'Snoopy, Snoopy, Snoopy.' He shook his head before slowly closing the door. 'And what do I owe this pleasure?'

Dominic's throat was arid. 'I know. I know all about you.'

Costa removed his coat and placed it on the bed. His movements seemed drunk, but his voice was very sober, deliberate. 'You do? Tell me what you know, Dominic, because even I do not know all about me.'

Dominic watched as Costa sat down on the edge of the bed, his arms folded, waiting.

'You're no war hero. You're a cheat. You didn't lose your leg in Vietnam, did you?'

Costa smiled. 'Did I ever say I lost my leg in Vietnam, Dominic? Did I tell you that?'

'No . . . but you gave people the impression, all over town, in the bar. You even let my . . .' His voice trailed off.

'Your mother? Did she tell you I even mentioned Vietnam? I doubt it, because I've said nothing to anyone, not here, not in the bar – no one. They believed what they wanted to believe, not what I told them.' Costa was becoming angry. 'I came from Tennessee – if a man can say he came from some place – and educated in the fine art of economics. So you see, Dominic, I'm not even the ignorant "redneck" you all thought me to be. Would you classify that as a lie, also? I travelled all over this great country, truck-riding, discovering life. I rode all across the edge of Canada on freight trains and went painting the highest buildings and longest bridges known to man. I used to write for some well-known and respected publications. My articles were published from New York to Texas. Some of them were good . . . initially.' He smiled, but his eyes were those of a person who scans beaten dockets, hoping beyond hope. 'I had a draft-version of a book just about hammered together using a lot of songs I'd written, when it all got destroyed in a fire in west Philadelphia. Eleven years of hard word, devoured by flames and bad luck. After that, I decided to travel the world and write the best god-damn book ever to see print. I travelled the head and toe of America, from old Mexico to Chile, crossing to Cuba, finally arriving back in the frozen lines of Canada. There I boarded a rusted old whaler that barely floated, *The Ramrod*, which took me to Hamburg in Germany. That was when I lost my leg. A message from God not to hunt His creatures without feeling His wrath.' He smiled and Dominic could taste the bitterness in it. 'Are you happy with that explanation, Dominic? Is more needed?'

In a perverse way, Dominic thought it brilliant, almost romantic, that if ever one had to lose a leg then this was how it should be, struggling against God and Nature, not in some ugly common war. In another time or another place, Costa's explanation would have mortified Dominic. Not now. It was too late. The ruthlessness in Dominic hardened. Costa had allowed a lie to become real, never contradicting the rumours, allowing its strength to touch and hide him. Worse, he had allowed Dominic's mother to believe it.

Costa stood up. 'I'm sorry for all this talking, but silence has become a mean torture for me, these days. Your mother is a good listener.'

Dominic's face reddened and a tiny bubble of acid exploded in his stomach. He wanted to smash the grinning face. 'Is that all she is? A listener?'

'Of course. Why? Did she tell you something else?' asked Costa.

Dominic didn't speak as he walked towards the door.

'The pictures, Dominic? Perhaps you would like them as a souvenir?' said Costa, holding out his hand, the photographs resting on it. 'You could show them to your friends. Your mother might even be interested in them? Here, take them.'

Dominic closed the door, refusing the offer.

Over the next few days, Dominic noticed a profound change in the relationship between his mother and Costa. Costa went for longer walks, returning only in darkness, while his mother barely spoke a word, going to church each morning, probably asking God's forgiveness.

Costa has told her. She knows I know, thought Dominic. *Knows I know all the dirty dealing. Good. That'll teach her.*

But a smell began to follow his mother regularly, a smell Dominic had associated with his mother only on rare occasions, when money was not so scarce: alcohol. Dominic began to dread his mother smelling of mints which she used in a futile effort to camouflage the horrible stench of dead leaves that settled on her breath, of wine in all its degrading cheapness which transformed her into a mumbling, sobbing wreck.

It was embarrassing and he dreaded the neighbours finding

out. They would say she was like Larkin's mother and all the kids would make fun of him. But when he asked her to stop, she simply smiled a lying smile full of hate and said of course she would, anything for her dear beloved Dominic. 'The only problem, my dearest Dominic, is that I do not drink, and if ever you accuse me again, you'll not know your arse from your elbow.' She wiped her flour-stained hands nervously on her apron, which was covered with windmills and trumpet-headed daffodils swaying in the breeze. 'Do you understand, my dearest Dominic?' she asked, before hitting him hard up the face with the wet dishcloth.

Chapter Ten

'You sure know how to run. The smoke was comin' right out of your hole, you were runnin' that fast. I couldn't stop laughin'. We should visit my apostles more often. I need a good laugh now and again.'

Dakota and Dominic sat on a wall adjacent to his house, watching the neighbours. You never knew what you'd catch someone doing in the privacy of a room. It was good entertainment, provided you weren't caught.

'I'm glad you thought it funny. I thought my heart was goin' to collapse. I thought they were right behind me, and I never stopped until I reached the safety of my bedroom, boltin' the door behind me.'

She giggled and he loved it, loved knowing he could make her laugh – even if it were at his expense. She was beautiful when she laughed and he wished he could make her laugh forever.

'That's the real world, Dominic, simply the tip of a dirty iceberg waiting to melt, drown you in its filth,' said Dakota, removing a sandal from her foot.

Her tone was sombre as she removed a tiny bottle of nail-varnish from her bag and slowly – very deliberately – glazed each toe, transforming them into rose petals of crimson mirrors.

Dominic swore he could see his face staring back at him as he looked on in amazement at her boldness. 'Does your ma not say anything, about you stickin' that stuff on?'

'What stuff? Nail-varnish?' Dakota looked amused. 'Why? What would she say?'

'I don't know. I thought only women . . .' He quickly stopped, catching his words too late.

'Women? And what am I?'

Dominic blushed, making her laugh.

'I meant older . . . Forget it. I don't know what I meant.'

'I love seein' your face light up like a Christmas tree.'

She seemed in an approachable mood, so he decided to ask her a question that had been gnawing at him since first he saw her in the water.

'Do you remember that day at the lake, when you almost drowned me?'

Dakota laughed. 'You deserved to be drowned. Remember?'

'Those marks on your legs, where did you get them from? Did someone beat you? Was that the one whose blood you wanted to paint the sky with?'

She looked away from him, refusing to answer.

Before he could ask again, a light appeared in the upper-storey window and a flimsy shadow stood silhouetted in a rectangle of red and orange flickering lights. One of Dominic's neighbours – Brenda Corr – came to the window, looked for a moment at the two figures on the wall, before closing the curtain, leaving a sliver of light flickering in the breeze.

'I bet she's puttin' tons of make-up on that face,' said Dakota, none too kindly, erasing Dominic's question from her mind before applying another coat of red on her big toe, which she wriggled, drying it in the warm air.

'I feel sorry for her,' replied Dominic, knowing not to ask about the marks again.

'You feel sorry for everyone,' accused Dakota. 'She didn't feel too sorry for anyone when she used to win all those prizes.'

Brenda had been the recipient of numerous beauty awards and was "destined for greater things", according to local talk. But then, almost a year ago, her beautiful face was shattered in a car accident. Dakota said it resembled a stained-glass window from The Church of the Misbegotten. Some – though not Dominic– gloated at her "comeuppance". Secretly, they were fearful of her leaving – leaving them to wallow in their soul-destroying drudgery of failures and repetitiveness.

Once – not so long ago – Brenda had every single wish come true, nothing was impossible; all dreams were achievable. Now she had nothing but darkness and self-induced exile.

'We should sneak along the wall and have a look at the Phantom of the Opera,' said Dakota, smiling, knowing she was needling him. 'Get her to team up with that Frankenstein-friend of yours. They could have scarred tiny babies, if they got married. I'd love to paint a family of scars.'

'You shouldn't talk like that about Larkin,' replied Dominic, defensively. 'What did he do to you to make you hate him so much? Some day you might need pity from someone who will –'

'Pity? *Pity?* I don't need pity from *anyone*. Do you hear me?' The tiny bottle of varnish fell from her hand, smashing itself on the rocky ground below, drenching the sleeping stones in red.

When he didn't answer, she repeated with force, her eyes the colour of gunpowder.

'*Do – you – hear – me?*'

He imagined her throwing him off the wall, laughing as she watched his neck snap.

'Yes . . . I hear you,' he said, climbing down.

'Where are you goin'?'

He didn't answer. It was always better that way.

'I don't hate Larkin,' she replied, matter-of-factly, glancing in his direction, watching his reaction. 'In fact, the next time we meet, bring him with you.'

'Great. I'll let him know,' he replied, unenthusiastically. He knew he should feel better now that he no longer had to choose between either of them, but something told him Dakota had other reasons; reasons that would suit her and no one else.

Chapter Eleven

'I hear you've been fillin' every idiot's head with shit, tellin' them you're some sort of magician?' said Dakota, staring at the shattered jigsaw of Larkin's face, from across the table at *Gino's* café. 'I've seen insects like you before, pretendin' to be butterflies, while all the time you are all-consumin' moths, tiny fangs devourin', leaving nothin' in your wake.'

This was a bad start. Dominic had hoped Dakota would show a bit more restraint. After all, it was she who had asked him to bring Larkin along.

Larkin said nothing. He appeared amused as his straw played with an ice cube floating on top of his *Coke*.

'Well, don't try any of your magic on me. Understand?' said Dakota.

Dominic was indebted to the owner, Brewster Mallon, when he screamed from across the room, 'Hey, you three! Do I look like a waiter? Do you want these burgers or not?'

'I'll get them,' said Dominic, quickly volunteering, wishing he was in the library – any place but here.

'That's what you're afraid of, isn't it?' said Larkin to Dakota, as soon as Dominic had left.

'Afraid? I'm afraid of nothin', Magic Man.'

'But you said it yourself. People like me devour everythin', tiny fangs, munch munch munchin'. Greedy. Nothin' left. Nothin' left for *you*, you mean. Isn't that right?'

She false-laughed. 'You don't have a clue about me; only rumours from filthy mouths and tiny minds. That's your information.'

'You fear me because we are so alike, Dakota. You never thought it possible, did you, that there could be two of you? But we are twins. The only difference is that my scars are on the outside.'

She reached to slap him, but his voice warned her, 'I'm not Dominic. I pay back two for one. That's how I've survived this long.'

Dakota had been caught off guard. His quick reaction angered and bewildered her. She wanted to leave, but that would strengthen him; weaken her. She had plundered into something for the first time in her life that had left her uncertain. It had not been planned this way.

'Fries and burgers, anyone?' said Dominic, breaking her thoughts. 'Do you want another *Coke*, Dakota?'

'I think what Dakota wants is to see me perform some magic, Dominic.' Larkin bit down on his burger before swallowing a tiny piece. Steam surfaced in his mouth. 'Tomorrow night would be perfect. Bring Dakota to my house, along with Timmy.' He smiled across the table at Dakota.

'Timmy?' asked Dominic. 'Why Timmy?'

'Magic, Dominic. All the magic in the world . . .'

That night, they arrived at the back of the shop and were quickly ushered in by Larkin, who indicated with a finger on his lips not to make a sound. 'It's okay. She's sleepin'. But the less she knows, the better,' he said, indicating with his head the closed door of his mother's bedroom.

Once inside his own room, Larkin told the group to make themselves comfortable. The show would start in a few minutes.

'You brought us here to watch the TV, Mister Magic Man? I'm impressed,' said Dakota derisively.

'Funny you should say that, Dakota,' grinned Larkin, producing a wizard's hat from behind the sofa, and placing it on his head. 'Thought you would like this little touch, Dakota.' He winked at her, smiling at her anger. 'Timmy? Take some of those crisps on the table. Sorry they're only ready-salted, but they're free. Right?'

Timmy smiled and nodded. This was great. A party, everything free.

'Tuck in, you two. You're in your Uncle Larkin's. Don't be shy,' grinned Larkin, seeing Dakota's unimpressed face. 'And those forks on the table are not for eatin' with. We'll need them, shortly.'

Dominic joined in the munching, much to Dakota's disgust.

'Not hungry, Dakota?' asked Dominic, innocently, regretting it the moment she gritted her teeth at him.

For the next few minutes, all that could be heard was the crunch of crisps and the slurp of liquid. Timmy was making disgusting noises with his straw at the bottom of the glass.

A flash lit up the room.

'Smile!' laughed Larkin, a Polaroid camera in his hand. He took another one, then another.

'Let me try!' shouted Timmy, fascinated as the camera vomited out the instant picture.

Larkin handed the camera to Timmy, instructing him on its ease of use. 'Wait until I get on the sofa, Timmy. No point in a picture without the best lookin' guy in the room in it. Isn't that right, Dakota?'

Dakota said nothing, as Larkin deliberately squeezed himself between her and Dominic.

'Let Dakota wear the hat, Larkin,' said Timmy. 'You've had your turn.'

Larkin smiled. 'Perhaps the lady does not want her hair ruffled?' he removed the hat and slowly brought it to Dakota's head, gingerly, as if feeding a lioness.

'Go on, Dakota,' encouraged Timmy, never realizing how close he was coming to getting his balls crunched by one of Dakota's kicks.

No sooner had Larkin placed the hat on her head than she reached for his throat, squeezing it gently but firmly, a grin on her face telling him he had come this close to getting hurt.

The flash went again, and Timmy cheered. 'I've done it Dominic! Can you believe it? Look! Look at the three of you!'

Dominic smiled at his younger brother. The flash seemed to have broken the spell between Larkin and Dakota, who now moved quickly away from each other.

'Here we go, then,' said Larkin, switching on the TV. 'Grab a fork, each of you.'

They all did, except Dakota.

A crackly buzz emitted from the TV screen before suddenly lighting up the entire room. A conversation was in progress and the host was grinning at some remark made by his guest.

Suddenly, the guest leaned into the camera, his eyes transfixed, and whispered for everyone to come a bit closer.

As if hypnotised, Larkin, Timmy and Dominic moved slightly towards the TV, forks at the ready. Only Dakota had the willpower to resist.

'Not everyone is obeyin'. For my power to be at full force, I need complete obedience,' whispered the voice from the screen.

'C'mon, Dakota. He knows it's you,' said Dominic, smiling.

'Fuck off,' she replied, rage simmering in her.

'*Ssshh*, the lot of you,' commanded Larkin as an eerily quietness encased the room. The group became as still as ice sculptures.

'I want you all to hold up somethin' metal. A spoon, a fork . . . anythin' at all,' continued the whispering voice.

In unison, they held up their forks, inches from the screen's surface. Only Dakota remained defiant, sitting watching them behave like fools, her arms folded in disgust.

Dominic could feel the heat on his face and wondered if they would all go blind, being this close to the TV. Unexpectedly, he felt the slightest vibration on his wrist as the fork began to warm in his fingers. In total amazement, he watched as the fork slowly – ever so slowly – began to bend. Mixed emotions of fear and awe coursed through him, making him want to giggle with nerves.

'Fuck . . . this can't be happenin'.'

But it was, and he froze as the fork bent in a perfect arch.

'Look! Look, Dakota! He can bend forks! Do you believe Larkin, now?' screamed Dominic, triumphantly, as if it were Larkin who had just carried out this earth-shattering performance. 'See? Now tell me you don't –' Dakota was no longer watching the screen. Her eyes – like those of Larkin – had become fixed on Timmy, now convulsing on the floor, squeezing his head, his gaping mouth making torturous mumbling sounds.

'Timmy? Timmy, what the hell are you doin'?' shouted Dominic frantically, wondering if Timmy was simply messing about, seeking attention. But as the tears rolled down his younger brother's face and the screams became louder, Dominic realised he wasn't faking. Something terrible was happening.

Only when the blood poured out his young brother's nose did Dominic scream for help.

'Don't just sit there starin' at him! Get help!' Dominic ripped off his own shirt and quickly used it to tide the blood while Timmy continued to squirm on the floor, kicking like a fish captured out of water.

During all the commotion, Larkin walked slowly down the stairs to reach the phone. He appeared to be in no hurry.

'What is going on in my house?' shouted the muffled voice of Larkin's mother. 'Larkin? What are you up to in there?'

'Nothin', Mother. Go back to sleep,' shouted Larkin from downstairs. He slowly lifted the telephone receiver, and dialled.

Dakota knelt down beside the two brothers, saying nothing, studying the looks on each face. Her eyes moved slowly over each face, the impressions, the lines of terror and uncertainty.

'Stop starin' at us,' commanded Dominic. 'Get a blanket or somethin'. Now!'

Afterwards – many months afterwards – Dominic would think of that gaze, that look, that intense stare that made him think of wasps and their lethal sting. He would think about hares, all munching and happy, not knowing they had tasted their last supper, not knowing the smiling girl studying them would become their executioner.

'Ambulance on its way,' said Larkin from the door. 'Don't worry, Dominic, Timmy will be fine. Keep the faith and it'll all work out fine. Just fine . . .'

Dakota stared at Larkin, captured by his calmness and command of the situation, his lack of concern or panic. She was seeing a different person to the one she had first met. He wasn't like all the rest. She realised that now. Dominic had been right. Larkin did have power – though not the power Dominic so childishly believed. No, this was a different power, a power that she had tried to attain for herself so painstakingly over the years. It was the power of fear, of playing on human weakness and superstitions, the power to keep them all in its chains.

Larkin met her gaze and smiled.

Chapter Twelve

'Told you he had power,' said Dominic to Dakota as they sat near the lake.

'How is your brother?' she asked, indifferently, trying to change the subject.

'The doctor thinks he's goin' to be okay. The metal plate in his head had been buckled, but the doctors said this had actually strengthened his skull. Do you want to know somethin' strange? I wouldn't tell anyone this, but you're different. Timmy used to piss the bed, every day.' Dominic felt his face go red, but continued, 'Well, he no longer pisses it. The doctor can't explain why, but I know it had somethin' to do with Larkin's power. That was why Larkin brought us there that night. Even though he laughed at me when I told him, I know deep in my heart that was the reason.'

'Will you stop talkin' like that? The only power he has is over weak people. Are you weak, Dominic? Is that what you're tellin' me; that because your pissy brother no longer pisses himself, I'm suppose to think Larkin is some sort of god? Grow up. I'm sick of listenin' about him. Anyway, I've got to go.' She rose, then turned and spoke. 'My ma has gone for the day. Do you want to come with me?'

It was a silly question. He wished for nothing else – ever. Just to be in her company, just the two of them. Everyone in the whole world destroyed. Even Larkin, if it came to it.

Ten minutes later, they reached her house.

Dominic had heard how poor they were, but the condition of the house shocked him.

It was little more than a shack that looked as if one good puff of wind would demolish it. To its left, stood a dilapidated barn where all the rags were sorted before being sold. It was a toss-up between house and barn as to which would collapse first.

His face told her every single thought in his head.

'You really are like the rest!' she screamed angrily, pushing him away, back towards the forest. 'Go on. Run back to the rest of the liars who think they are so good and fine. Go on! Get out of here!'

But he didn't want to run. Didn't want to face being away from her.

'I'm sorry,' he mumbled.

The fierceness of her face glared at him and for a second he expected a terrible kick. Instead, she simply turned her back on him and headed towards the large, tattered barn, as the dog in Dominic became a courageous wolf, nipping at her heels, awaiting a command.

No one in his or her right mind would have ventured inside the barn, seeing the haphazard state it was in. But Dominic did. He would have swallowed that barn whole, had she commanded.

Piles of rags, sorted by their textures, lay haphazard against the walls. A rusted weight machine, bags and hooks stood alongside them. Over near the back entrance, stood an old table, an army of jars and paint brushes sitting quietly on top minding their own business. To the left, a mixture of homemade painting frames stood neatly stacked against the wall. A few were covered in old bed linen.

For the next few minutes, Dakota went about the table, arranging what needed no arranging, hitting empty jars so hard some broke, splintering into great lumps of ice.

He wanted to say something to calm her, but the wolf was a now a scrap-yard dog, spineless, eyes downward with guilt.

'I'm sorry, Dakota, for the way I looked when –'

She bristled. 'If you say sorry one more time, you really will be sorry. Understand? You're becomin' more pathetic each day. Your ma should have named you Sorry, instead of Dominic. You probably said sorry the moment you popped out of her cunt in the hospital.'

Dominic was speechless. A mouse could have nested in his gaping mouth.

The angry quietness lasted for minutes, before she acknowledged him. 'This is one of the reasons why I brought you here,' she said, pulling dusty linen from a lone picture over in the corner. 'I don't really care any longer if you like it or not.'

He walked towards the picture, trepidation in his stomach. He knew it would mock him, but he wouldn't show his hurt.

'Well?' she said, impatiently, her arms folded.

He couldn't speak. It was uncanny. Not some childish line drawing, but a perfect rendering; almost a photograph in its reality, and as beautiful as any over in Syracuse Heights.

'*Well?*' she snapped. 'Say somethin'.'

'I . . . can't believe it. It's . . . fantastic.'

'What's wrong? You don't like it. I can tell. Should I've made you more handsome?'

As soon as Dominic saw the painting, he knew he had lost her. He wished to God she had made him ugly, a caricature. He should have been delighted, but he was no better than the rest of the town. He hated her because he realised God had given her the Gift and this would be her ticket out of this stinking town, leaving him with his dreams of being a lawyer or a journalist, because that was all they were, an idiot's dreams. He would never be able to escape. He had known that all along, but now he was forced to taste the truth and it tore his gut. His heart told him that this was her real reason for bringing him here. She was letting him know that things had changed, forcing him to face the coldness of that reality.

'No . . . it's great. I love it,' he lied, kissing her quick, void of emotion. It was a Judas kiss, terrible in its unforgiving anger and filled with the enduring chill of rusted hope.

Without warning, a tiny creature ran over the top of his toe, stopping a few inches from him.

'Fuck! A rat!' He tried kicking it, but it was gone, replaced by two more. He wanted to run. He felt they were crawling all over him, climbing up his legs, munching on his balls. He imagined his face ripped in half, the rats' buck-teeth chewing his nose off, leaving him as disfigured as Larkin.

'They'll only bite you – not kill you. Stand still. Stop being such a coward!' She was disgusted with him.

In a minute, they were all over the place. He wondered why he hadn't spotted them as soon as his eyes had focused in the light. They made his skin crawl but he was determined to steel himself.

'Now you know how I got the marks on my legs,' she continued. 'I've been bitten so many times by them, I'm immune. I was too ashamed to tell you at the beginnin', but now I no longer care. You're not worthy of me. You'll never be.'

'How can you say that? I love you, Dakota.'

She began to laugh. 'Ah, yes. I had almost forgotten that. Love love love. Shit shit shit.'

There was something buzzing in his head. He thought about wasps, again.

'Why are you sayin' this, Dakota? What did I do?'

'*Do?*' she smiled a horrible skin-tearing smile. 'Nothin'. You'll *never* do nothin', Dominic. Don't you see that? I made a mistake – one that I will make sure of never repeatin'.' She clenched her fists, angrily, so tightly her knuckles became the colour of snow.

He would not stop her. She could punch his face to a pulp. He wouldn't flinch. He'd show her how strong he really was, how much of a man he could be. All he needed was the chance to prove it.

When the punch came, it wasn't physical. 'I won't be seein' you again, Dominic. It's over,' she pronounced in a perfect, impassive stillness.

The air was being sucked from his lungs. He found it difficult to breathe. A heaving mass of water, thundering in his skull threatened to drown him. He wanted to fall at her knees, beg forgiveness, but someone was squeezing his head in a vice, tightening it with each turn of the handle. The wasps were in his mouth, eating his tongue. He couldn't talk. If she deserted him, he would die. He would kill himself.

'Goodbye,' said her voice, void of emotion. It sounded metallic in his head, a stranger's voice; one he no longer recognized. 'Don't ever come back here again. It won't be safe for you.'

A few seconds later, the sound of the barn door closing broke the spell, allowing him to gasp for air. He was alone with a terrible silence, a mocking silence, making his hands shake terribly as he staggered out like a punch-drunk boxer, a has-been who should never have been a contender in the first place.

Chapter Thirteen

'What are you doin' here?' asked Larkin, stacking bread on top of the shop's counter. 'Shouldn't you be with Dominic, countin' the stars, filling his head with nonsense?'

Dakota stood in the doorway of the shop, a large green folder under her arm. She ignored the cynicism. 'I may have been wrong about you.'

'An apology? From you? Now, if you don't mind, I'm busy . . .'

'Where's your mother?'

'None of your business.'

'Have you ever thought about why all the adults in this town are so fucked up? Do you think it's the water?'

'I never think about anyone in this town. The less I think about the town, the better I feel.'

'I have a theory. Want to hear it?'

'No.' He pushed her away, before turning the light off in the back of the shop. 'I'm closin', so if you don't mind . . .' He gestured with his hand, showing her the door.

'Inbreeds. The whole town. Your mother is no different from mine – so don't try to hide it.'

Larkin grinned. 'You must think I'm as easy as Dominic, windin' me up. Why are you wastin' your time – and mine? Don't you realise by now that I'm above that? I'm the one who fucks with minds. You don't even come a close second.'

Now it was her turn to grin. 'I'm the only one with the courage to tell you to your scarred face that your mother's a junkie and that you encourage her habit so as to keep her under your control.'

For a moment, his features registered a slight movement.

He shook his head. 'You know nothin' about my mother – *nothin'*.'

'Really? Do you *really* believe that? Tell me now, lookin' straight into my eyes, that you believe that.'

Larkin felt a swelling in his lip. It was turning arid, asking to be licked. He resisted the temptation, knowing how it would look.

'Tell me that woman upstairs, pretendin' to be your mother, doesn't inject herself daily with the god of dreams,' continued Dakota. 'Lie. Tell me that she has protected you every day since your face was savaged, that she wasn't ashamed of you since birth. Go on. What are you waitin' for? Or are you as predicable and pathetic as Dominic, believin' in fairy tales and pots of gold?'

He glared at her, feeling his fists ball angrily, waiting to punch, knock out her grinning teeth.

Slowly, as if dealing a winning hand of cards, she placed the green folder on a table. 'Open it.' She smiled, daring him.

He remained immobile.

'You'd be surprised what fantastic secrets our tiny, insignificant library holds,' said Dakota, opening the folder, its newspaper-clippings haphazardly spilling over her feet. She picked one up from the floor and read it slowly, torturing him, watching delightfully, as he tried in vain to steel himself. '"*He knew everything, Larkin Baxter. He instilled fear, but so subtle you hardly realised it, until it was too late, touching you right on the* shoulder. *You couldn't take a shit without him knowing its weight.*"' She placed the page in front of him. 'That's what one of your neighbours reported to the police. Did you know that?'

'You've overstayed your welcome. If I were you, I'd leave right now,' said Larkin, his face impassive.

'Leave? The thought never crossed my mind. Besides, I haven't even come to the juicy, wuicy parts yet.' She cleared her throat, deliberately loud, before continuing. '"*The tests resulted in a distorted picture. The reason being the subject's manipulative power – something that should have been spotted by a competent psychiatrist. Unfortunately, Doctor Stoppard's ineptitude and unsophisticated method prevented a clearer, more authentic report. It is now evident that the subject, Larkin Baxter, was fully in control of his state of consciousness, never losing voluntary power of action or thought, pretending to be highly responsive to suggestions and directions from the hypnotist. Mark my words, given the chance, he'll kill again.* Confidential report, highly critical of the administration's doctor in Allenwood Mental Institute, who supported the release of the accused from the institute on the grounds that he believed he posed no threat to society."' Dakota stopped reading. 'Was it the boy who threw acid in your face that you killed? Is that why they put you in the mental institute?'

'Nothin'. All that effort for nothin'.' He looked at his watch. 'Nine minutes of the most borin' time of my life, and what did you achieve with it? Nothin'.'

'Playing hard to get? But I was keepin' the best for last. So lets make it an even ten. What do you say?' Before he could answer, she continued her reading. 'This has got to be the best: "*I hated that boy from the moment he was born, tearing out of me with those bloody little hands, ripping me in half, entering the world with a grin, all bloody and shit. My anger of him was equal to Eden's God. Anger, that over the years, turned to unadulterated hate. It wasn't my fault what he turned out to be. Blame God. He created the monster.*"'

'Don't push your luck with me. You don't have a clue as to

what I'm capable of doing. Understand?' He watched her, as if from a distance, intent and silent, as she inched towards him.

She came closer, scanning her eyes over his face, studying how the scars criss-crossed into tiny boundaries, ploughed like acres of sweaty clay. 'Oh, I think I do know what you're capable of. But the question is, do you? Do you know what you are capable of? Really capable of?' She pried open his fingers, and placed something in his hand. It felt cold to his touch. It was a knife. 'You once said that we were twins and that I feared you because we are so alike, that the only difference between us were the scars: yours on the outside, mine inside. Remember?' When he didn't reply, she hissed, *'Remember?'*

He felt cornered, trapped, just as he had been trapped that day when he crashed through the window, destroying himself forever.

She brought his hand up to her face, the knife touching her eye. 'Do it,' she whispered. 'Rip my face in half. Scar me, make me ugly like you.' She pressed the knife deeper into her skin, just below the eye, piercing it. A teardrop of blood trickled down her cheeks. 'Do it. Don't be a coward like Dominic. *Do it.* Think of that so-called mother of yours, tellin' the world how she hated you from the day you were born. Do it. *Do it now.*'

He could never remember having this feeling, an almost tingling feeling of fear zipping in and out of his body, confounding him further as he brought her hand away from her face, forcefully removing the knife, watching it fall to the ground.

The room was void of all sound, like ice melting in a glass as he brought his thumb up to her face, cushioning it tight against the tiny wound she had made, stemming the flow of blood.

She, in turn, traced the lines on his face, as if her feathery fingers could erase all the pain and anguish. 'All better. Healed. Gone forever. Chased,' she whispered, leaning to him, kissing his nose, his lips, his shattered face. 'Better, better, better.' Dakota smiled, a smile so powerful and perfect he would have murdered just to see it again as she exposed one of her breasts fully, resting his head on it. 'Breathe it in, deep, down to your lungs.' The smell from her was seeping through his head, confusing and exhilarating. 'Remember that smell always. It will never let you down, never betray you – always love you.' She felt the hotness of his breath on her breast. 'Suck,' she commanded, softly yet firmly, placing a nipple on his lower lip, resting it there, as his teeth hovered over it, resembling a tiny guillotine. Her test of will and strength, of cunning and understanding, a test that would decide, once and for all, who between them held the greater power. But would the Magician succumb to the Witch's mystery and all her wet and wonderful darkness? Or would he see through her, decapitate the teasing nipple, the bait, spit it right back in her face, laughing at her for being so stupid as to think he could be defeated so easily, just like Dominic?

The taste was the most beautiful thing imaginable. He thought he would suffocate in its beauty as she ran her fingers through his hair, her fingers pulling tightly, clamping his face to her breast.

'Good boy' she soothed, relieved, watching him feed greedily like a little pig at market. 'Good . . . good boy. That's right, suck nice and long.'

He couldn't hear her, couldn't see the awfulness in her eyes, never understood, until it was too late, her whispering into his ears: 'Now we are one, my little boy. I'm the mommy, now . . .'

Chapter Fourteen

Two weeks would see the summer end, and as far as Dominic was concerned it couldn't end quick enough. The first couple of days after the rejection from Dakota were the worse that he had ever experienced. He couldn't eat, couldn't sleep, questioning every word he had spoken, every action he had taken and still he could not figure it out. Why? What terrible thing had he done to make her hate him?

He hadn't seen Larkin about, either, and guessed it was the shop. Larkin usually took over when his mother was feeling "ill".

Dominic watched as some of the kids in the street played skipping, while others entertained themselves with a battered football. He envied them, their friendship for each other; their loud laughs that screamed: look at us everybody!

Some of them probably had girlfriends. The thought made him more depressed.

'Things can't be that bad? You look as if you're about to be executed,' said Larkin, smiling, a cigarette in his mouth.

Dominic hadn't noticed him coming up the street.

'So, you're still alive? Thought you'd left town.' Dominic was glad Larkin had made an appearance. It was good to be in his company.

'I'm sorry about what happened to you and Dakota.'

Dominic felt embarrassed by the remark, wondering how the hell he knew. Was she bragging all over town that she had dumped him? Who else knew? Was that why everyone grinned when they saw him?

'Nothin' to feel sorry about,' replied Dominic, angrily. 'Anyway, it was me who dumped her when I saw the way she lived, like some dirty tramp out in the woods, in a shitty shack that stinks like dog shit. Fuck, you only have to look at her clothes, all the hand-downs from her ma's rag store.'

He hated her now, more than ever, hated her blabbermouth. He had been just a plaything for the summer, something to kill her boredom. 'I hate her,' he said unintentionally out loud.

'You'll probably hate me even more when I tell you she asked me to take her to the movies on Friday.'

Dominic was gutted. He could not believe what he was hearing. She had never asked him to take her to the movies. Not once had she asked. He would have loved that.

'Take her. You're welcome to her.' He realised he was shaking with anger. 'But watch you don't get nits from her. I did. And if you kiss her, the smell of her breath will –'

Larkin laughed. 'I told her no.'

Dominic was stunned. 'What? Why? Don't you like her, either?'

'She doesn't bother me in the least. I simply told her there was no way I would let her come between you and me.'

Dominic felt humbled. Had the shoe been on the other foot, he knew he would have chosen Dakota over Larkin. He felt as if he had betrayed his best friend, and for some girl who simply discarded him like dirt. Despite what Larkin said, Dominic knew that anyone – especially someone such as Larkin, his face disfigured – would love to be seen with Dakota. He wondered if Larkin had performed some sort of magic for Dakota, mesmerizing her despite her self-confessed loathing of him?

'No, I . . . I want you to take her, Larkin. Really. This will let her know she means nothin' to me. Not now – not ever. You'll be doing me a favour.'

Before Larkin could reply, Dominic noticed that all the kids in the street had stopped playing and were all staring at his house. Above him, John Costa appeared at the window of his room, staring down at the street. He was completely naked.

'What the fuck is he doin', the dirty bastard? Flashin' his cock at all those kids?' asked Larkin, pointing his cigarette towards the window.

The kids were all laughing, shouting at Costa to show his hairy dicky-joe.

'Dicky-joe, dicky-joe, show us your dicky-joeoooo,' they sang in perfect unison, like little angels in a choir.

'I've got to get the fuck up there,' said Dominic, rushing towards the house. 'Find out what the hell he's up to.' But before he could make another move, the sound of breaking glass froze him to the spot as the entire window came splintering down upon the street, showering the ground with its contents.

Adults emerged from houses, wondering what the commotion was all about.

Everyone in the street seemed powerless as the naked Costa climbed out the window and descended awkwardly down the battered drainpipe, his false leg gleaming for all to see. Thin leather straps held the false leg, precariously, to his upper torso.

Perhaps it was the heat; perhaps the pain in his missing leg drove him, but as he reached the ground he stood glaring at Dominic and there was no doubt in Dominic's mind that Costa had gone mad and if he could only get his hands on a knife he would put it to good use, probably on Dominic, plunging it straight into his head.

'I *am* a war hero!' he screamed at Dominic. 'I am!' The row of war medals were pinned to his bare chest releasing a ribbon of blood which mingled perfectly with them. No one seemed to have noticed how bizarre the medals looked, attached to angry skin, dangling from side to side. They were too fascinated by the nakedness of the one-legged man struggling to keep his balance on such shaky foundations of wood and plastic.

'Would you look at his leg, the pervert?' someone whispered, and automatically everyone stared at the false leg, its greasy yellowish plastic gleaming as the sun tore down on it.

'Must've got it in *Woolworth*,' someone shouted, making everyone laugh. 'He must've thought he was the *Six Million Dollar Man*, the speed of him coming down that drain!'

They were all at it now, making jokes.

Innocent faces had now turned vile with hate, and suddenly, without warning, Costa pushed through the crowd, attempting to run up the street, out of their way. But the mob was having none of that and quickly pursued, shouting at him, at his leg, his nakedness, his awkward manoeuvres and clumsiness.

Dominic followed the horde, fuelled with hatred for Costa, for the feelings towards his mother and for trying to replace his father.

'Mad man! Mad man!' shouted the kids, some of whom started to throw stones at the staggering figure. One or two tried to trip him up, hoping to capture him before he could escape the street. They didn't know what they would do with him once he was captured – but they would do something. There was little doubt about that. They couldn't have perverts running about naked, bringing disgrace to their street's good name.

Only Larkin watched from a distance, captivated by the madness, watching how quickly the animal is willing to be released. If only he could harness that animal instinct, bottle it and force it to act on command instead of impulse, if only . . .

It was strange how one tiny sound could rise above the rest, above the howling and screaming obscenities of the mob, but rise it did, louder than their combined mouths could muster. It was the sound of wood and plastic snapping, like a twig in an old horror movie as Costa went tumbling to the ground, his false leg breaking in two perfect pieces. It made the most sickening sound Dominic ever heard and suddenly the entire street went silent, watching as the naked man struggled to pull himself up.

Twice he groped for support from a wall; twice he went back down, flaying his skin in the process, causing tiny rips to bleed. Only the medals remained defiant, clinging to his skin for dear life.

Silence. Absolute silence. Only the groans of pain from Costa could be heard. Then the whispering started again, followed by a few giggles, soft at first but becoming louder, braver in numbers. Someone was about to make a comment, a joke about what do you call a naked man with one leg, when suddenly the voice of Dominic's mother sliced right through.

'Shame on the lot of you!' she screamed, pushing through the mob. 'Scum. Every last one of you. And as for you . . .' she glared, staring directly into Dominic's eyes, as she struggled to pick Costa up. 'I'll speak to you later . . .'

She was only half the size of Costa, but her anger lifted him, carrying him back to the house, deliberately leaving the false, mangled leg in the street, an indictment to them all.

'That was the best entertainment I've seen in ages,' said Larkin smiling, as Dominic returned. 'We'll have to get Costa to do the Great Escape every week.'

'It wasn't funny,' replied Dominic, subdued.

'No? You were leadin', right at the front, lappin' it up.'

Now that calmness and sanity had returned, Dominic felt nothing but shame for his actions. No excuse could be made, and he didn't offer one.

'I better go in. Fuck knows what's waitin' for me. I'd be as well to get it over with.'

Larkin stopped him, just as he entered the doorway. 'Before

I forget, what's that old barber like, the one who lives in your house?'

'Kane? He's hateful. Hates the world. Smacks the fuck out of my head, every fuckin' time he spots me. I wouldn't mind seein' him knocked down by a bus.'

Larkin laughed. 'Good. We should get on like a house on fire, him and me. I start summer work in his shop, next week. Clip clip. I'm gettin' fed up practically runnin' our shop on my own. My ma's treatin' me like a slave, takin' everythin' for granted.'

Dominic shook his head in disbelief. 'You're mad, workin' for him. He's evil and hates everyone – especially kids.'

'Yes, and he's just right, hatin' kids. So do I.' Larkin grinned. 'Can't have them about me. Told you, Dominic – time to grow up. That's why I'm finished with school. No more crap from those bastards.' He playfully blew the smoke into Dominic's face, before strolling down the street, leisurely, not a care in the world.

That night in bed, as Dominic tossed and turned with guilt, chalky headlights lit up his room and a car purred softly in the dark. He could hear voices whisper and his mother crying as the door of a car slammed, making his wish come true but filling him with self-loathing.

Costa was gone, but the memory of him would remain in Dominic's head many years later, in the dead of night when man is prey to his truths, when the unpleasant lurid intentions and guilty secrets begin to emerge from their subconscious slumber.

Fifteen

The static from the old projector crackled like webs being burnt while its beam exposed a blue-speckled mass of smoke, swirling about in mesmerizing spirals.

Christopher Lee stalked menacingly in the shadows outside the old inn, his bloody eyes scanning the darkness, zooming in perfectly to the naked neck almost 20 yards away.

There was something curiously compelling about the victim's repulsively fat head nodding heavily on a fragile neck. She resembled a dying flower.

All the girls in the audience sat glued to their seats, ghosts hidden in their eyes, their hands tightening against a boyfriend's arm. They couldn't stomach what was coming next – the teeth, the blood, the dead – as the Prince of Darkness prepared his coup de grace before quickly slipping soundlessly away into evaporated fog.

Dakota wanted to slap them, shut that stupid screaming out. They were like slaves, clinging to their master, hoping for mercy to be shown.

There was one annoying girl sitting directly in front, with a silly hairstyle that simply asked to be set on fire. It looked like a haystack, and the thought of it bursting into flames made Dakota smile, just like Christopher Lee as he plunged his mouth neck-wards, shaking his head for good measure as the *Brylcreem* from his greasy head gleamed in the moonlight.

Dakota hated sitting here, in this decaying movie hall with its urine-stained seats, pretending to be afraid, pretending to enjoy Larkin's company. But it would be worth it all in the end. She would bet her life on that.

Twenty minutes later, the lights came on.

'Did you enjoy it?' asked Larkin, as they stood with the crowd waiting to get out.

'A bit scary. Luckily, I had you to save me from that monster,' replied Dakota sarcastically, smiling as she gently touched his back, easing him towards the doors and into the faint light.

Outside, the night air was cooling quickly. There was a warning in it of summer's end and dark nights coming that would stretch forever. Rain was only a matter of minutes away.

'You know, you still haven't told me about your scars, how you got them,' said Dakota, breaking the silence as they walked. 'I've only heard the rumours. Even those reports revealed little. I want the truth. I want to know. *Now!*'

The question was full of brutality, without a hint of mercy. Yet, that was why he found her so intriguing.

When he didn't acknowledge her question immediately, she continued, relentlessly. 'They said your mother did it to you, one night in her drunken dreams.' Her face was expressionless, but he knew she was smiling, mocking. 'Said she used acid as she staggered from room to room. Or a boy did it. But that's not true, is it? No. Acid would have melted your face. Wouldn't it?'

No one ever had the audacity to ask him that question, in that tone, and he realised that this was all part of the Great Plan that had floated in his head, rudderless, without direction, until now.

'Sometimes it is good to explore the boundaries,' he replied. 'Other times it can be dangerous.' He stopped walking, turned to her, pushing her hard against the wall, the thud of her body sounding like a book falling in an empty room. He knew he had hurt her, but she didn't utter a word, only equalled the measure of eye contact, smiling, balancing her smile with his grin: challenging him.

How could he not want her, this strangest of creatures, even though he knew she was toying with him, manipulating him just as she had manipulated poor, insecure Dominic?

'Let me tell you this one secret,' whispered Larkin, into her face. 'My mother never drank in her life. Not one drop. People in this fuckin' town are so ignorant of other people's behaviour, they simply pigeonhole it because their simple brains are as small as a pigeon's. Anythin' more complex than eatin', shittin' and pissin' confuses them.'

That was lovely, thought Dakota. *A raw nerve exposed, and me with the tiny hot needle, pushing it further in.* 'Forget I asked,' she said, feigning anger. 'Perhaps you and Dominic are not so different. You have the same pathetic mentality. You deserve this town – both of you.' She pushed him away. 'I'm goin' home. You keep your little town, you and Dominic. I've bigger things planned; things that would make tiny, pathetic brains explode like fireworks lightin' up the night. So you just be careful, little boy, I wouldn't want yours all over my face.'

He watched her walk angrily down the street, stiff and uncompromising as iron. She was powerful. Perhaps too powerful. 'Okay!' he shouted, his mood suddenly changed. 'I'll show you . . .'

From the street corner, Larkin watched as tiny bugs bounced off the street light with its amber glow attracting them like drunks to whiskey.

One more cigarette, he told himself, as the cig butt tumbled to the ground, joining a family of others that littered his feet like spent ammo. The nicotine had failed to ease the urgent pain in his head inflicted by sudden memories.

Larkin's reluctance fascinated Dakota, but she said nothing fearing she would destroy the completeness of his torture, wanting to capture this moment, never spoiling its conclusion.

'It's been a long time. I'm not even sure if I can still get in. Probably like a fortress now. Look at the size of those locks.'

Enormous rusted locks, each the size of an apple, were studded to the door's bulky frame.

He sounded nervous, unsure, but she was wary of it. What if it were an act, waiting for her to drop her guard? She looked to meet his gaze, but his face was a ghastly parody of the face she had seen an hour ago.

'No. It can't be done. This was all fucked up from the beginnin',' he said.

'Find a way,' she whispered, softly but with command. 'We're not leavin' now. We've come too far to run away like headless chickens, like Dominic, like all the scum in town.'

Resigned, he went around to the back of the old shop, hoping for an opening of some sort, questioning whether he actually wanted to discover an opening to his worst nightmare of festering pus and twisted animal corpses.

He looked about for something hard, a piece of pipe, strong wood – any item that would help pry open an old wound in the shop's decaying body.

An old piece of bicycle frame was his best hope and he tore at it, breaking it down to something suitable for his needs. Sweat was clinging to him, but her mocking voice propelled him.

The sound from the house was faint, but he had heard it clearly above the night sounds of the street. He stopped moving and placed his ear to the door. There was someone – something – moving about. Rats? Birds? He cursed his heart for banging so loudly.

A few moments later, all was still again. The silence was starting to twist his thoughts. He envisioned shadows moving about like liquid scents fighting with each other, hoping to capture him. He wished he had not come. The sounds of the night became different now, somehow deeper, louder and more threatening.

Suddenly, the door opened and he almost fell through the gap.

'Boys! You send them to do a man's job . . .' Dakota stood at the door, grinning madly, covered in dirt and laced in cobwebs. Her jeans were torn and he could see blood on her legs glistening in the yellow light. 'You want to see the look on your face, Larkin. And what is that smell comin' from you?' She laughed louder now, tears mixing with her sooty face like cheap mascara.

It was an accusation, and he resented it; resented her standing near him, that smug, cruel shape of her mouth, purposely avoiding any pretence of not wanting to hurt him.

'C'mon,' she said, not waiting. 'Time to kill the dragon.'

The hallway was dark, looming with silhouettes as he stepped inside. He stared at the endless formation of wooden ribs, the floor de-crucified by time and wear. Sparse light filtered through the corroded roof, teasing him with its delicate movement. A musky smell rose from the ground and entered his nostrils. He felt a slight twinge in his stomach. All these years the smell had remained, unchanged, redolent, reeking of shit and piss. For a split second he saw himself running in slow motion, his feet crushing skinny bones and rotten flesh covered in feathers.

'Well?' asked Dakota, touching his shoulder, making him shudder.

'In there, the tiny room off to the left.' He pointed and she quickly grabbed his finger, pulling him along, playfully but with malice.

Perhaps it was instinctual, his body acting without his expressed permission, but he no longer resisted, and felt a tingling in his spine from the same touch that was now dragging him.

'Don't be afraid. I'll make it all go away,' she whispered, grinning at him.

He knew she wouldn't make it go away. If anything, the opposite would become the truth.

Hordes of flies stretched across the floor like giant slabs of tar, feasting on shit and flesh. As Dakota and Larkin approached, the insects ascended as one massive and filthy vortex, swirling in their faces.

'Fuck off!' shouted Dakota, spitting them out of her mouth. 'I hate flies. Small and annoyin'.'

'A bit like Dominic?' said Larkin, removing some of the insects from her hair.

They both laughed, nervously, breaking the suspicion each had for the other, if only for the moment. They shared it for a frozen tick of the clock, and a tiny flash of understanding passed between them that even though they were different in so many, many ways, they were also a perfect one: full unity, deceiving all.

'Tell me,' she asked, softly, so concerned. 'Tell me what happened, every tiny detail.' She kissed him gently on the lips, so gently he did not feel it, then placed her hands on his shoulders, slowly forcing him to the ground. 'Tell.'

He licked his lips, searching with his tongue, as if she had left a secret message on them. 'I was six at the time – Silly Six, my mother called me – when I climbed in through one of those windows, hoping to find somethin'. I don't know what, perhaps it was simple curiosity, but as soon as I entered I knew I had made a mistake. I thought someone was here, in the dark, ready to cut my throat, feed me to the rats . . .'

Dakota listened intently, like a child at a fireside story, watching his lips form and shape every word from his pattern of memory.

When he ended his story, she simply said, 'That's it? That's what you've been hidin' from? Are you sure you're tellin' me the truth, the whole story? Perhaps someone did get you, perhaps your memory refused to remember what he did to you. It wouldn't be your fault, what he did. Tell me.'

'I don't know what the fuck you're blabberin' about. I wish I hadn't brought you here.'

She seemed disappointed, as if she had been betrayed. She believed he was attempting to deceive her, unfaithful to the evidence surrounding them. She hated deception – with the exception of her own – but even this, she knew, would be revealed someday, willingly or not because, she also, had made a belief out of lying.

'I preferred the acid on the face story. Much more interestin',' she said, smiling, her eyes contradicting it.

'Sorry it didn't live up to your expectations,' he replied, sarcastically. 'Perhaps if I had lost an arm or a leg, you would have found it more to your taste.'

But Dakota was no longer listening. She was bent over, staring at a window covered with a few strips of wood.

'Was this the window?' she asked.

Larkin looked bemused. 'How the fuck would I know? It was years ago. I don't even know –'

'Think! Was this the window?' She pulled him towards it.

'Could be . . .'

'Help me get this wood from it.'

'Okay,' replied Larkin, laughing. 'What are you goin' to do? Make me jump through again, just for your perverse entertainment?'

'That,' she said pointing at the gaping teeth of glass, 'is blood . . . ' A thin film of dust covered a slightly dull pink-looking stain. Dakota blew gently on the glass, removing much of the dust. 'It *is* blood, Larkin. Your blood. There is no other answer.'

Larkin felt dizzy. 'It can't be. Not after all these years. It's probably blood from birds, rats . . .'

'You *know* it's your blood. No creature's, no ghost's, no denyin'. You *know*.'

'I'm leavin',' he said, not moving as he watch Dakota lick greedily at the glass, the dampness from her tongue distilling the pinkish encasement, bringing the dead fluid to life.

'I've . . . I'm goin', Dakota. I can't stand this, what you're doin'.'

'For you. I do it for you. Don't you see? I've freed you. This dragon can no longer harm you. I've slain it for you. Only for you . . .'

He attempted to rush from the room, tripping, falling, staggering drunkenly in the dark. The room was becoming claustrophobic, trying to drown him. It had waited all these years to destroy him. Now it had won.

'Fuck you, Dakota!' he screamed, looking for a gap, an escape hatch of light, as he clawed at the door, pulling it apart, shredding his fingernails in the process.

He fell to the ground, outside, gasping. Air never tasted so good. He sucked it in desperately, like a desert thirst, cursing her over and over again. She had shamed him, exposed his weakness. She would tell. He would be detested, just like Dominic, a mockery.

The thought of being exposed became a damp patch sticking to his head. He tried desperately to ignore it, but the more he tried, the larger the patch of thought became, threatening to cover his entire head like a disease. There was only one remedy for the patch of malignant thought. He knew what must be done, knew he would have to go back in, seek her, find her, and prevent her from exposing his secret. He would have to kill.

'Dakota? Dakota!' he shouted, entering the dark, protected by the sound of his voice. 'Where are you?' *Nothing. What if she's gone? She could be far away, laughing, running her mouth, telling secrets never meant to be told.*

He thought he heard something, over to his left. Rats? Old Mister Rootree?

'I knew you'd find me. But you're too late.' She held out her arms as if to hold him, and only then did he notice the slick sheen that clung to her face. 'Dakota – what have you done?'

She didn't answer. The bloody sliver of glass that lay beside her did all the talking.

'Ah, fuck . . .' He couldn't believe what he saw. Dakota's face shredded beyond recognition, blood poring from it.

Larkin fell beside her, tearing at his shirt, desperately trying to halt the flow of blood from her face.

Suddenly she uttered a sound, barely a whisper, but it reassured him. 'Don't you see, Larkin? Your blood and mine, minglin' for eternity? The glass from the window, joinin' us together, for always? Ugly but beautiful.' She laughed her dark and cynical laugh.

'*Sshhh*,' he whispered, tightening the cloth. 'Easy. You're goin' to be fine, Dakota. Do you hear me? I'm not goin' to let you die. Do you hear me? Nothin' will ever harm you again. Do you hear me?'

She nodded, weakly, drained of all fight and hope, before resting her head in the shadow of his body. *What a fool. As if I would need you to protect me.* She smiled to herself. Things had worked out better than planned.

Chapter Sixteen

'So, you've come at last?' said Kane, scissors in hand, clipping perfect shapes from the flawed head of a customer. '9.00 sharp you were told.'

'What do you mean? It's only gone one minute after,' replied Larkin, entering the barber's shop.

Kane glared at him. '9.00 sharp. Not a second before; not a second after. But not to worry because the next time you decide to sleep on in bed, don't bother coming back. There are other boys out there looking for extra pocket money.'

A stone of fear moved in Larkin's stomach, sliding downwards like acid. He was not interested in the money. He was after something far more valuable.

'Here,' said Kane, handing him a brush. 'Get that floor spotless. At 10.00, make sure my tea is ready. I take it strong – no milk or sugar. And make sure it's hot.'

Larkin spent the remainder of the morning sweeping puddles of hair, making tea and ensuring he kept out of Kane's way, unless instructed to do otherwise.

As the day neared its end, Larkin had to admit there was something about the shop, something snugly mysterious with its emporium of treasures: sweets harboured in jars lined the groaning shelves; towers of comic books piled haphazardly, waiting to collapse; shrunken, rubber heads dangled ghoulishly from the nicotine ceiling while religious paraphernalia, consisting of Lourdes water housed in limpid images of Mary and old bibles from Kane's colporteur days, sat incongruously with magazines of half-naked women, decapitated corpses and Mafia rub-outs – appropriately enough – in barber chairs. A *Brylcreem* poster of Denis Compton, cricket bat in hand, proudly proclaimed: *Perfectly set for the day.* Even the smells of soap and lather seemed to mix perfectly with the acrid stench of singed hair and body odour that poured from the sweaty clothes of the customers.

Occasionally, Larkin wiped the mirrors on the walls, keeping his eyes glazed, as if in a trance, not seeing his face. It had been years since last he saw his face; he doubted if he would ever look at it again.

Over the coming days, he watched the barber's every move, especially when Kane would remove the large mahogany box that once housed Cuban cigars, from beneath the sink, opening the lid, releasing the aroma of dead tobacco and exposing an intricate, nacre-handled cutthroat bedded on blue velvet.

This is what it's all about, thought Larkin, as he watched Kane, razor in hand, quickly attend the soapy face of Mister McCarthy, allowing the soap to settle but not congeal.

'Never allow soap to congeal,' said Kane out loud, knowing Larkin was watching, fascinated. 'If it congeals it closes the pores, the stubble becomes like nails.'

There was something about this boy that made him different from the rest of the dirt in the street, thought Kane, as he watched Larkin observe him. He's keen. Those scars have given him strength and the patience of observation.

Expertly, Kane made a swathe in the air with the lethal metal before resting it on the pliable neck of a customer, Mister McCarthy, whose protruding Adam's apple was the size and shape of a robin's egg. With a slight, invisible movement, he removed the peppered-black soap, leaving McCarthy's cheeks gleaming a reddish pink, not unlike a baby's bum.

Power, thought Larkin, watching the stubble vanish. *To make something disappear, with such ease, is true power.*

Kane's voice broke his thoughts, surprising him with its leniency. 'One day, you will be able to do this – with discipline. You can become the best barber the town has ever known – better than me, perhaps.'

Larkin said nothing. He wasn't expected to. Kane made that perfectly clear from day one. But it suited Larkin, this wordless relationship. The less spoken, the less revealed.

'Turn on the radio,' commanded Kane, abruptly, glaring at Larkin, annoyed that he hadn't even smiled, acknowledging the praise. 'You should know by now what to do when it's near 3.00.'

Larkin reached over and turned on the crackling voice of the old Bakelite wireless. Its static nipped at his neck as the classical music of Puccini's *Madame Butterfly* floated about the shop, appreciated only by Kane who prayed for the last pangs of day when he would sit, upstairs, listening to his beloved music collection. He didn't trust leaving the collection in Missus Tranor's, and so was always late returning to her house, telling her how a customer had belatedly walked in, just as he was about to close the shop.

Once, Larkin slipped up the stairs, hiding in the shadows and watched as Kane placed a record on the player and listened to the tragic love story of Mimi and Rodolfo in *La Bohème*, tears rolling down his face as he hummed in perfect harmony.

Larkin was fascinated. How could music make a person cry? He could never remember anyone crying, least of all his mother when she witnessed his destroyed face.

And why would she cry for you? asked a voice indistinguishable from Dakota's. *We're not here to listen to music and lies. Have you forgotten?*

'No. I remember.'

'Who's there?' shouted Kane's voice, apprehensively. 'Is someone out there?' He went to investigate, but found nothing, only the night breeze corkscrewing its way up the stairs to greet him. 'That stupid boy. Doesn't he know how to close a door?'

From across the street, Larkin watched as Kane closed the door, shaking his head angrily, before venturing back up the stairs.

'I remember,' whispered Larkin, stepping back into the shadows. 'I always remember.'

Seventeen

'What could you kill?' Larkin asked Dominic as they scanned the lake for Charley Blue Eye, a pike gone mad.

Dominic thought back to an incident two years ago when, walking though the forest, he accidentally disturbed a nesting bird. Without warning, the bird flew at his face, frightening him. His reflexes swiped at the bird and he hit it, accidentally, cracking its skull. He remembered how the bird convulsed, looking at him for mercy to kill it. He couldn't, dreading to touch it, so he left it jerking in the grass, and ran home.

Two years ago, but still it haunted him.

'I could kill any creature,' he replied with false bravado.

'Hmm. Any? Like a fly? Could you kill a fly?' asked Larkin. 'Like the old woman who swallowed?'

Dominic didn't even have to think about that one. 'A fly? No problem.'

'A rat?'

For a moment he hesitated. He thought about the rats running all over Dakota's barn. 'Yes.'

They laughed. This was a mad game, but it would kill a few minutes while they waited for Charley to poke his head up out of the water. They both had clubs resting on the bank, but doubted if they would get the chance to use them. Charley hadn't lived so long for being a fool.

'What about a dog? A nice wee dog like the one Maggie Nelson owns? Even Mister McCarthy's Sheeba?'

'A dog? That's cruel.'

'*Could you?*' persisted Larkin. 'Could you kill a dog?'

No. Of course he couldn't, but he was determined to win this mind game. 'If it attacked me. No problem.'

'A monkey? A wee hairy monkey? Eek-eek!' Larkin started doing monkey impressions, hunched over, his arms trailing the ground. 'Could you or could you not kill a monkey?'

They were laughing louder now. 'You're sick,' replied Dominic. 'Know that?'

'You still haven't answered my question. Could you stiff a monkey?'

'What? Where the hell would you get a monkey?'

Larkin smiled. 'In the zoo, stupid.' Something was happening to his features.

Dominic stumbled. 'Perhaps . . . if the crunch came . . .' Dominic knew he couldn't and the hesitancy in his voice exposed him.

'Chicken!'

'Don't call me that. That's what that little tramp called me. I don't want to be reminded of her.'

But Larkin was showing no mercy. 'Could you really kill a monkey? Yes or no?'

'I'm gettin' tired of this.'

'Answer me. Or else you join Charley.' Larkin wrestled Dominic to the ground. 'I mean it. I'll throw you in.'

'Okay, okay! Enough! If I had to, I could. I know I could. Satisfied?'

Dominic was glad when they finally decided to pack. The

game had become too weird. Old Charley was probably grinning at them from beneath the water as they made their way back up the hill.

It was two days later, on a Thursday afternoon, when the local radio station carried the horrific story about the break-in at the local zoo. Someone obviously possessed, had attacked the zoo's monkeys, wounding three, killing two. One of the chimps had been decapitated.

People were shocked as well as outraged. It was hard to believe that someone from the town could do such a barbaric act. Outsiders were the perpetrators, more than likely.

Only Dominic thought different.

Larkin simply laughed, saying it was a coincidence, and he wished to hell he hadn't opened his mouth if this was what was going to happen every time he joked, being accused by his best friend.

Chapter Eighteen

The summer gone, Archangel Secondary School reopened, filling its corridors with dejected pupils, with death-row faces. Dominic hadn't spoken to Larkin since the day he questioned him about the attack in the zoo, over three weeks before, and he wondered if, perhaps, they were no longer on speaking terms. *Probably Dakota poisoning his mind, turning friend against friend*, he rationalised.

He returned home from school and the moment he walked in, seeing his mother motionless on the sofa, wiping away tears, he knew something terrible had happened, knew it was his father.

'Well, look who's here. My big son, the one who just loves his mommy to death. Isn't that right, my big son?' She had been drinking and her slurred words frightened him.

'Come over here, my big son.' She patted the sofa.

Reluctantly, Dominic obeyed, sitting down beside her. He didn't want to hear what she had to tell him.

Without warning, she attempted a kiss on his lips, burning his mouth with the cheap brandy wetness on her lips.

'*Keep away from me,*' he shouted, pushing her back against the sofa. 'I can't stand you when you're like this. You're disgustin'.'

Since Costa's departure, her depression had become more acute, making her more irrational. At its worse, the depression made her pick at the wallpaper with her fingernails, leaving them a bloody mess and the walls devastated like leprosy. Neighbours had begun to talk about her, the state of the house, the empty bottles of wine and brandy at the back of the house. He couldn't help but notice the blood dripping from her fingernails and the blood smeared upon the wall, its paper curled in tiny shreds.

'What's happened? Why are you drinkin' at this time of day?' he asked quickly, dreading her reply, knowing her answer would devastate him.

His mother slowly turned her head towards him. 'He's dead. Electrocuted . . .'

Dominic felt tightness in his chest as the blood drained. 'No! My da's not dead! He can't be! You're lyin', trying to scare me!'

His mother looked at him angrily, before wiping her face. 'Your father? You stupid boy. Not *him*; it would never be *him*. I'm talking about poor Mister Kane,' she replied, starting the crying again. 'He was shaving himself in the shop . . . a loose wire must have touched the water in the sink . . .'

Kane dead? Dominic couldn't believe it. His prayers were answered, and it brought such great delight that he wanted to believe in God and all His goodness. More importantly, his father was alive.

'That's terrible,' he said, hoping she wouldn't see his grin. 'The poor man. Electrocuted . . .'

'I've no more lodgers. What will I do? What will happen to us.'

Dominic found the defeatism in his mother's voice peculiar. There was no obstacle insurmountable for her; no problem that could not be solved, eventually, by the quickness of her calculating mind. Was she losing faith in her own ability? He doubted it. She would weather then defeat this crisis, just like she always did. She was Napoleon and Genghis Khan, rolled into one, invincible and uncaring. She was simply looking for sympathy from him, but she'd wait a long time for that. A very long time, indeed.

As he turned to leave the room, his mother hit him with the bombshell.

'After the funeral, you'll be moving into Mister Kane's room. You'll be there until I can find another lodger – and you better hope I find one soon.' Suddenly, she was as sober as a judge, her face fierce, prepared for battle.

Dominic had been right, seeing no sympathy coming her way, she reverted back to her old self, a killer queen looking for vengeance.

Kane's room? The thought made his stomach percolate. 'Why can't I stay with Timmy? He's stopped wettin' the bed weeks ago.' Panic was in his voice,

'You did nothing but whine about the poor man when he was alive, how you wanted the room for your selfish self.' His mother looked at him with disgust. 'Well, Dominic my darling, I'm your fairy godmother and your wish has just been granted. Immediately after the funeral, you'll be moving in. If you're lucky, perhaps Mister Kane will come and visit you – now get the hell out of my sight!'

Two days later, Dominic reluctantly entered the room which seemed to have retained the presence of Kane: a drawer full of moth balls and mints released an offensive stench into the air; a set of false teeth, grinning, floated in a whiskey glass filled with dusty water. A forest of snuff had filtered onto the carpet and was so overpowering it made him sneeze each time he touched the carpet with his shoes. Even the old lodger's bed had retained the shadowy cavity where he had once slept.

It was well into the night before Dominic could muster enough courage to gingerly slide into the bed, dreading the touch of the sheets with their stench of Kane's dry sweat, toenail clippings and flaky skin.

Freedom had its price and Dominic's youthful imagination made sure he would pay in full. A car lit up the room for a second, turned the dark into chalk, then was gone; high-heels clicked outside in the street and a woman, drunk and loud, laughed, making the hairs on his neck stand. And when he desperately tried to avoid the centre of the bed and its stink of dead Kane's sweat, something kept pulling him back, back into the shadowy cavity which was as deep as a grave. In the cold storage of his mind images were conjured up magically; dark and disturbing images of winged things and sparrows with severed tongues reaching to kiss him. He kept thinking of a foot in a bag and a strange boy old before his time, of Joey Maxwell and Aunt Kathy laughing with Kane. He wanted to run out of the room, but was too ashamed. His mother would never let him live it down and Timmy Blabber Mouth would tell everyone. Larkin would piss himself laughing and Dakota would snidely comment what did you expect from Dominic?

For one terrible moment, he thought he could hear asthmatic breathing close by, like whispering from a dead mouth touching his ears, teasing him to panic. Someone – some*thing* – was in the room.

When he awoke, he was drenched in fear. It was still dark outside but the reveille from the milkman's bottles calmed him, reassuring him it was now morning, the ordeal over for now.

There *was* something dark lurking in the room – he was convinced of that – something that had been captured by his mind and his mind alone, something seamless, thick with terror.

Chapter Nineteen

Larkin waited for Dominic to get out of school, surprising him with an offer to go to *Gino's*, just like old times.

'I suppose you're sorry you're out of a job, now that Kane has died?' asked Dominic, as he and Larkin sat, sipping *Coke* and eating chips. It really was like old times.

Larkin smiled and Dominic remembered the smile from way back when he first met Larkin and his horrible greasy foot, and just like that day in Ryan's, this smile was a secret yet to be told.

'No, I'm far from sorry. Actually, truth be told, I was there when it happened. I watched him sizzle like a sausage on a fryin' pan. It was incredible. His hair was the last thing to melt. Even his false teeth took a bit of a batterin'. It was a beautiful sight.'

Dominic fidgeted nervously with his chips. 'You're jokin'? Right? You were there? You saw it?'

'Are the Hulk's balls green? Why do you never believe what I tell you? I told you that if you wish for them, dreams could come true.'

'What? What are you on about?' Dominic sipped at the *Coke*.

'Kane. You wanted him dead. It happened.' Larkin snapped his fingers. 'Just like that. See what faith can do, the power?'

There was a lump, like a stone covered in dust, sitting in Dominic's throat. 'I didn't want him dead,' he laughed, nervously. 'People say things like that, stupid things when they're angry. I know you're windin' me up.'

Larkin studied a chip before slicing it in half with his teeth. 'Am I? You hated him, didn't you?'

'Yes, but . . .'

'It's okay, then. Don't say a word.' Larkin placed his finger on Dominic's lips. 'I understand.'

Dominic could feel his heart pump in his ear, swelling his face. 'I didn't hate him that way,' he mumbled. 'I didn't . . .'

'Look, the bastard's dead. Wishin' and regrettin' will change nothin'. Right?'

'But . . .'

'Right?'

'I suppose so. But aren't you afraid?'

'Of what?'

'Of someone tellin' the cops, of you goin' to jail, executed?'

Larkin laughed. 'They don't execute kids, Dominic. In fact, they make excuses for them. Besides, who would tell the cops? Where's the proof that it was anythin' other than an accident? That's the wonderful thing about magic. People don't believe. Yet, it's all around us, at all times, invisible, watchin' over us, waitin' to help, if only we ask. Many are called to believe but few are chosen, Dominic. You can be one of the few, if only you truly believe what power *you* possess.'

'I couldn't even keep a girl over summer. So much for my power.'

They laughed, finished their meal and stood to go.

'Talkin' of girls and magic . . .' Larkin reached behind Dominic's ear. 'Hey, presto!' An envelope was produced.

'How the hell did you do that?' Dominic could still be amazed by the simplest of party tricks.

'Faith, my friend. Simple faith. Now, for somethin' more important . . . ' Larkin tore open the envelope. 'Ta la!' He removed two tickets from the envelope and playfully slapped Dominic's face with them.

'What are they for?'

'Just two tickets to the *Limelight*, meals and drink included. And girls. Lots of them. Real girls. Not like the bunch of pimply scarecrows runnin' around here.'

'The *Limelight*? But you won't get in there. It's for adults.'

Was the other ticket for Dakota? He dreaded the thought of asking.

'Adults? Dominic, Dominic, Dominic.' Larkin shook his head. 'If you think like a kid, a kid you'll remain. Anyway, I can hypnotise the bouncers, make them see what I want them to see, guaranteed. Not only will I get in, but you, Cinderella, are comin' to the ball, also.'

'Me? I thought the other ticket was for –'

'Thought wrong. Didn't you? Meet me at 9.00 sharp, outside *Mullan's Bakery*. That is, of course, if Mother permits you.' He laughed. They both did.

'Let her try and stop me,' said Dominic, full of confidence, not feeling an inch of it.

The night started ominously for them as they missed the bus by a few minutes. The next one wouldn't be coming for at least another hour.

'What do we do now?' asked Dominic.

'We walk.'

It started to rain – the first in a week – as they commenced the long walk to the *Limelight*. Dominic had the strangest feeling in the pit of his gut that something was trying to prevent this night out.

'We're goin' to be soaked to the skin, and by the time we get there it'll all be over,' complained Dominic, pulling the collar of his jacket up to his neck. 'Maybe we should head back, leave it for another night?'

'Are you kiddin'? Do you think I can get these tickets anytime? Anyway, we'll get there. I know a shortcut that'll cut our time in half. Let's run.'

They ran until they came to the waste ground of the local scrap-yard, of its burnt-out vehicles and elephant's graveyard of metal and glass.

'Looks kinda spooky,' said Dominic, reluctantly continuing.

Larkin laughed. 'You're a bit big to believe in ghosts, Dominic, wouldn't you say?'

They entered the yard, and the noise from the rain beating on metal became thunderous. It felt like being inside a submarine, one that had just been torpedoed.

'Oh, fuck . . .' whispered Dominic, spotting the figure that he dreaded more than anything in the world. 'It's Nutter.'

Dominic stopped, rooted to the spot. Nutter was nestled between the carcass of a smashed-up Ford and a crate, bottles of wine at his side. The rain had turned torrential, but Nutter seemed immune to it, to his surroundings. 'We have to be careful. If that crazy bastard spots us, we're dead meat. He looks like he's drunk, into the bargain. I knew we shouldn't have come this way, Larkin. Let's head back and catch the next bus.' It was almost a plea.

But Larkin simply laughed out loud, shouting, 'He's only as crazy as your mind allows. Isn't that right, Nutter?'

Nutter stirred, focusing his eyes on the two dark figures in front of him. 'What? Who?' asked his slurred voice.

'Why'd you do that?' asked Dominic, incredulously. 'We could have sneaked to the other side. He wouldn't have spotted us. You don't know what the hell you've done.'

But Dominic was wrong. Larkin did know. Knew exactly. 'Magician never sneaks!' he shouted at the top of his voice. 'I have the power!'

Nutter smiled and for a moment Dominic thought that perhaps the drink had dulled his senses, confusing him. Perhaps things would still work out. But he was wrong. Nutter was a reptile, and the speed at which he grabbed Larkin was startling.

'You disfigured little bastard,' hissed Nutter, squeezing Larkin's throat, tightening the grip as he banged Larkin's head hard against the Ford's door, causing burnt, flaky metal to land on his hair like metallic dandruff. 'Where's your power? Eh? Magic, my hole! I should have fixed you in school, before you got this cocky. And where's your wee weasel friend? Eh? Everyone in school knows you two are fuckin' each other, and tomorrow the whole town will know. I'll make sure of that. I'll tell them all I caught the two of you with your panties down to your ankles.' Nutter's strength buckled Larkin to the ground. 'Gonna tell me where your friend is? I was right, wasn't I? He's run away like a little girl. Shits his panties, as well.'

Dominic hadn't run away. Perhaps he should have. Larkin had brought this madness on himself. No one else could be blamed. But instead of running, Dominic hid between the shadows and mangled metal, terrified, praying that a miracle would happen.

'Oh, I'm sorry. Am I hurtin' you?' asked Nutter, squeezing Larkin's neck tighter with his vice-like grip.

Yes, he was hurting him, but Larkin did nothing to fight the beast, simply smiled, welcoming death. Even when his eyes were falling somewhere in the back of his skull, he refused to defend himself.

Fuck, thought Dominic, more terrified than ever. *Larkin believes his magic power will save him. He's going to die. Nutter's gonna kill him. Then he'll go after me . . .*

Dominic would never forget the look on Nutter's face, an animal going for the kill, as he reached for an evil-looking piece of sharp metal to plunge into the dormant Larkin.

Any moment now, Larkin would be dead, and unless Dominic fled, he also would become a victim, beat to a pulp by this maniac. But each time he thought about running he saw an image of Kane sizzled like a sausage. Dominic knew in his heart that Larkin had killed Kane, killed him because of Dominic's hatred of the man. Dominic may not have wanted the man dead, but he was responsible not only for his death, but for turning Larkin into a murderer. He owed Larkin. Big time.

Without thinking, Dominic lunged at Nutter, grabbing him by the hair, hoping to pull him away. If it worked, they both could escape, have a laugh about it in *Gino's*. But his feeble action only helped to incite Nutter further, as the thug roared and threw Dominic back on the ground, telling him in no uncertain terms that he was next, what he was going to do to him.

A powerful punch from Nutter hit Larkin full in the face and Dominic swore he heard Larkin's neck break. What happened after that would haunt Dominic eternally.

Standing up with all his force, Dominic slammed Nutter's head, as hard as he could, against a protruding piece of metal that had been the car's fender. Dominic would never forget how Nutter's blood shot up and outwards, like ink from a fountain pen, splattering his face with force as it escaped from the impaled head.

He had wanted to stop watching the ghastly scene, but he could not draw his eyes away from the magnetic horror as he fell to his knees, mesmerised by the revulsion, sobbing, covered in blood.

There was a sickening sound of flesh being torn as Nutter slowly craned his neck in Dominic's direction. He seemed to be trying to pull his head from the protruding metal.

'Oh, fuck . . .' whispered Dominic, as Nutter's eyes came to rest directly in line with his own terrified eyes. Softly, Nutter's right hand began to twitch and slowly the fingers began to creep along the ground like a tarantula, towards the defeated Dominic who lay exhausted, unable or unwilling to move.

'Keep away from me . . .' The fingers touched Dominic's leg, tightening their grip, squeezing down to the bone, sending tiny bolts of shock into his marrow.

Then the movement stopped as the hand went limp, leaving no doubt in Dominic's mind that Nutter was dead.

At that moment, Dominic felt so alone, utterly, beyond redemption and afraid to be afraid, breaching the depth of his bones with the terrible knowledge that there would be no resurrection for Nutter. No Lazarus. No miracles or magic. Nothing, only a stifling darkness that came at him from all sides, crushing him in its tight grip of death and despair and he just wanted to go home.

Float, he told himself. *Float way up to the moon, the smiling moon with its knowing wink.* But he could no more float than he could turn back the hand of time. His knees began to shake and he detested them for their weakness.

'It's okay. It's okay, Dominic. It's over. Breathe in . . . easy now. Easy.' Larkin's voice was soothing, reassuring. Above them, the moon broke through murky night clouds as the sky's canopy suddenly became raw, the colour of chopped liver and purple ink set on fire, creating a chiaroscuro of a circus; a carnival of strange and beautiful creatures from God's own manic zoo. Larkin was smiling at him. 'I told you I had the power, Dominic. Remember? Power that can be yours – if only you believe. Power that can turn even Nutter into dust and mangled bones. Well, that's all he is, the bastard. Dust and mangled bones. And you, at last, have the power, a power that will remain with you forever. But we've got to get out of here now, Dominic. Do you understand?'

Dominic could see Larkin's mouth move but the words were out of sync, like a foreign movie badly dubbed with b-actor voices.

'Come on. That's right. Take my hand. Easy. You're goin' to be okay. We'll go to my house, get you out of those clothes,' said Larkin, easing Dominic up from the ground.

'Yes . . .' mumbled Dominic. The smell of blood and oil was overpowering. It made him think of his father, slaving away in the darkness, mocked by all.

'Now listen very carefully, Dominic. This never happened. You and I alone will have this secret. No one must ever know. Do you understand?'

Dominic steadied himself before answering. 'We're even. Do *you* understand, Larkin?'

'Even? What do you mean?'

'For Kane. The debt is paid.'

Larkin looked at him strangely. 'For Kane?'

'I know you killed him, killed him because of me.'

For a second, Larkin did not reply. Then he said, 'Yes, okay – we're even, Dominic. Now, please, lets get the hell out of here, before some nosey bastard spots us.'

Two hours later, Larkin returned to the scrap yard, alone, like a dog returning to its own vomit. He had waited until Dominic had gone home reassuring him that all would be well, not to worry about a thing. He would take care of it.

Nutter's battered body remained untouched, hidden from view. The nearest house was over a mile away. Thankfully it was Sunday morning. The yard would remain closed until Monday. By then it would all be over.

Larkin removed the cutthroat from his jeans and sat down beside the body. He prized Kane's lethal utility as much as his old models of Frankenstein and the Werewolf.

'Ladies and gentlemen, for my next trick, I will amaze you by makin' my great friend Nutter disappear before your very eyes.' He patted the body lovingly on the head then, one by one, he began to slice off the fingers, placing them into one of three bags he had brought with him. 'This little piggy went to market . . .' he sang, as each finger was removed. Bending, he removed Nutter's boots, and began working on the toes, journeying all the way upwards towards the genitals. He removed them, and placed them in a separate bag, eventually to be accompanied by the eyes. He wondered what Knocked would have looked like, scarred like him for life, how he would have coped. Expertly, he sliced the face, until it was barely recognizable as human, and quickly set about the removal of all protruding items beginning with the ears and finishing with the nose.

'Much better, Nutter, if I say so myself. A great bloody improvement.'

Four hours later, Nutter was spread evenly between the three bags. Larkin thought about keeping the head in the fridge, at the shop, but decided against it. He didn't want to give his mother a heart attack.

At least, not yet . . .

Standing, soaked with sweat, he grinned at the bags. 'Ladies and gentlemen, thank you . . .' In his head he could hear the applause of approval, people cheering, screaming for his autograph. 'Not to worry,' he shouted back. 'There'll be more entertainment for you later . . .'

'Larkin? Is that you? Have you been out all night?' shouted his mother as he entered the shop from the back entrance. 'Where's my medicine? You know I need my medicine.'

He ignored her grating voice as he set about fixing the "medicine", mixing it with four spoonfuls of sugar to satisfy her sweet tooth. He was still covered in blood, but he knew she would hardly notice. She hardly noticed anything, these days.

'There you go, Mother. Beat that down your neck.'

She didn't care for his tone, his choice of words, but she didn't argue with him. She seemed too tired to care, and just so long as her "medicine" was nearby, she could tolerate his intolerable behaviour.

'You've been gone all night. Where have you been?' she asked, fixing herself comfortably in her favourite chair.

'Where have I been?' He smiled. 'I've been to London, to see the Queen, while I rode my cockhorse to Banbury Cross. I've even a seen a cow jumpin' over the moon, tonight, Mother, but no matter what I've seen, I'm sure it's not half as mad as what you've seen.'

'How can you speak to me like that? I'm your mother. Have you no shame?' She was trembling with anger.

'Careful, you don't want to spill that expensive "medicine", do you?' He leaned in, whispering in her ear. 'You thought you were so slick, didn't you, stealin' *my* morphine during your visits to the hospital as I lay there in agony? But it has all come back to haunt and punish you. Hasn't it, Mother? Now you can't live without it, addicted for always.' He laughed, making her cringe. 'Perhaps it's Eden's God, all angry at you for watchin' your son screamin' in agony, cryin' out for just a tiny spoonful to ease his pain? Perhaps it's Morpheus' way of showin' you that he is the one in charge of your Eden, and no other gods you shall have before him? Eh? *Eh!*'

She jumped at the sound of the last word. 'You used to be . . . such a good boy, Larkin. Please . . . I'm very sick.'

There was silence in the room, as he walked behind her, touching her hair, stroking it. 'I'm sorry, Mother. I don't know why I say the things I say, they just seem to spill out of me. And after the shock of seein' Mister Kane all burnt and smokin' . . .'

'Please, Larkin, don't remind me again of how that poor unfortunate man looked. I know it must have been terrible, but you've described, in detail, so many times how the man died.' She shuddered. 'Can you please not mention it anymore?'

He nodded, sadly. 'It's just that I had my heart set on becomin' the best barber in the world, but now I'm finished. I'll never become one.'

She patted his hand, clumsily, hating the coldness of his skin. 'You don't need to become a barber. The shop will always take care of you. Don't you know that?'

He left the room and immediately she regretted her words. It seemed so easy to upset him. She wished she hadn't opened her mouth. Thankfully, the medicine was beginning to work. All aches in her body were slowly being erased. There was a nice softness floating in her head; a softness that she wished would last day after day. A few moments later, she felt her body relax, float from the chair. She felt happy now; terribly happy.

Larkin returned a few minutes later, carrying a small bowl, a towel and other utensils.

'What are you doing?' asked her startled but subdued voice.

He smiled. 'You shall have the privilege of being my first customer.

'What? Don't be silly. Wouldn't we look the proper ones sitting here covered in soap, you with your plastic razor trying to shave a couple of my hairy moles?' She tried to lift her hand, to push him away, but the medicine was now in full control. She could hear her own voice, but it seemed strange.

'But it's the only way I'll prove myself to be the new barber. I know I can be the best, with your help. Don't you want to help me, Mother?'

'I suppose it would do no harm,' she said, reluctantly, seeing the look on his face.

Gently, Larkin applied soap to his mother's face, kneading it, like dough mixed with milk.

'And how are you today, Mister McCarthy?' he asked, taking on the role of a barber.

A nervous smile appeared on her face. 'Don't be expecting a tip from me, young man, unless you do a good job,' she said, her voice hamming a masculine throaty gruff.

'Oh, no sir! You will never forget this shave. Like a baby's bum.'

'Larkin! Watch your language.'

Larkin, watch your language, mimicked a snide voice in his head. *Larkin, rub soap in those scars of yours. That'll take them all away, all on a summer day. Remember how she neglected to look after you, the day you entered old Rootree's, all on your own? Had she being doing her job, that day, as a so-called mother, perhaps you wouldn't have these scars for the rest of your life – nor her crocodile tears.*

There were times when he tried – and succeeded – to keep these terrible feelings for her consecutive, allowing each a life of its own, each dominating the other in equal periods. But most times the darkness ruled, bullying out the decency that he knew he possessed but hated for its weakness. He thought the darkness like ink seeping destructively into bread, destroying all that was good in him.

The voice was laughing now. *I hated that boy from the moment he was born, tearing out of me with those bloody little hands, ripping me in half, entering the world with a grin, all bloody and shit. My anger of him was equal to Eden's God. Anger, that over the years, turned to unadulterated hate. It wasn't my fault what he turned out to be. Blame God. He created the monster . . . created the monster . . .*

He felt his fingers tighten on the razor and something bubbling in the hollow of his stomach.

'What's that music you're playing?' asked the mother, the soap tickling her nose. She felt a sneeze coming on.

'Opera. *La Bohème.* It tells the tragic love story of a poor poet, Rodolfo, who falls in love with Mimi, a seamstress.'

'I didn't know you knew about opera?'

'There are quite a few things you don't know about me, Mother.'

He found her skin not unlike the naked chicken he practised on. It was withered, beyond care and he wondered if the consumptive-ridden Mimi's skin was as horrible.

Her skin may be withered, sneered the voice, *but at least it isn't scarred.*

He tried to ignore the voice as he watched her eyelids becoming heavy.

Why should you have all the scars? whispered the voice, as blood moved faster and faster, pumping in his brain.

He placed the razor on her throat, just below the chin line, and slightly cut her skin.

It was strange and powerful how such a tiny nick could

create such a forceful release of blood. Her clothes would be ruined, but it was a small price for freedom.

She hadn't even stirred, lost somewhere in the music of dreams and failed hopes.

He made another nick, a fraction wider to the left of the original, and watched as the blood joined her blouse, spreading over it like watercolours in rain.

She moaned, this time, but he held her hand tightly, giving her strength, the strength *he* had needed all the years of his isolation inside bandages and darkened rooms.

Outside, the silence of the morning became eerily beautiful, like a symphony performed by ghosts of fallen warriors. *La Bohème* came to a crackling end leaving only his soft breathing in the room.

He looked back at her, before closing the door, thinking how she resembled one of his models, stiff yet life-like. He tried to think which model, but it wouldn't come to him.

It was only later in bed, as he closed his eyes, squeezing them tightly, feeling his lids flicker as if housing angry ants, did he agree with himself that perhaps a barber's life was not for him. There were other journeys to be made, other realms to visit and discover, other possibilities to be tried.

He wished he could go now on this fantastic journey, but he needed rest. Tomorrow he would set out, gather his followers and together they would conquer all. He would reveal new magic, new potions and unbelievable feats.

But that would come tomorrow . . .

Chapter Twenty

Saturday mornings always attracted Dominic to the local bar. Outside, crates of empty beer bottles were pyramided, their smell fermenting in the early sun, their contents gone with last night's dreams. Flies, vile and lazy, nestled on the crates and buzzed angrily at their hangovers.

'Whaddye want?' asked the barman, scrubbing-brush in hand.

'Nothin'. I'm just lookin'.'

'Then go look elsewhere.' He hated anyone watching him struggle with the vomit that permeated the ground, staining it like great maps of the world.

'Not want me to kill the flies for ye?' Dominic asked, showing him the newspaper rolled into a policeman's baton.

The barman stared at him for a few seconds, then skyward for Divine guidance.

'Okay . . . but don't eat them.' He grinned, but Dominic only nodded solemnly, turning to the task of transforming fat-bellied flies into perfect inkblots.

A dog came to watch then, bored, sniffed suspiciously at a dead bird, its anorexic legs protruding like miniature branding irons.

From across the street, Dominic could see a neighbour's son waving frantically.

'Your da's lookin' for you!' screamed Terry McGlone.

Terry loved giving bad news. The more distressing, the happier he became. 'He's shoutin' all over the place like a mad man for you. Looks like you're in for it!'

To see someone "in for it" could bring tears of joy to Terry's eyes. He was practically wetting himself with glee as he escorted Dominic back down the street, like a guard, fearful Dominic would escape justice.

Terry was a local bully, but an unusual one because he had a conscience and only hit the other kids when they deserved it – which was usually twice a day, except on Fridays when he got his pocket money. He never touched them on Friday. A decent bully, really.

Tiny knots formed a rosary in Dominic's stomach as he peered tentatively down the street for his father.

'There's your da, now,' grinned Terry, pointing at the figure in the doorway. 'I bet you're shittin' yourself.'

'Where've you been? Didn't I tell you not to be going away from the door?' His father was standing beside Timmy. 'Get your coat and let's get goin'. We're late.'

Terry was devastated. That was it? A few words? Not a kick up the backside? Not even a slap on the head for Dominic? For a moment, it looked as though Terry would complain to Mister Tranor about his misguided leniency towards Dominic. Instead, he simply walked away, head down, mumbling about a wasted journey down the street.

'For heaven's sake, will the two of you cheer up a bit? It's the hospital; not O'Neill's we're going to.'

O'Neill's was the local undertakers, but as far as Dominic was concerned, there was little difference between them and the dreary wards of the hospital where his mother had been rushed to, almost a week ago.

As the trio entered, a soft breeze rallied the combined stenches of piss, vomit, lemony-ammonia and the dry-talc smell of death, filling the corridors with the universal dread of all hospitals.

'How is she today, doctor?' asked Dominic's father.

The young doctor was scanning a pad.

'A slight improvement from yesterday, Mister Tranor. We hope to give her some soup, later. She had some tea last night, but couldn't hold it down for long. It's a slow process.'

Dominic's mother lay motionless in the bed, her pallid complexion as one with the linen sheets. It wasn't her first attempt at suicide, but it was her most imaginative as well as elaborate. Instead of simply opting for an overdose, she had decided to slash both her wrists also. This time she almost made it, having been pronounced DOA by the doctor on duty. Only the attentive eyes of an old nurse, who insisted the doctor perform a miracle, frustrated her effort.

It worked. She would live to die another day.

While his father signed some forms, Dominic bent and whispered in his mother's ear. 'You could've waited,' he accused. 'I told you my math results were due and that I would do well. But you don't care about anyone but yourself. Next time, I hope you die.'

Dominic knew his mother could hear every word he spoke, but she ignored him, feigning the death she had yet to perfect, like a log, stiff with shame, filled with loneliness.

For one moment, as his eyes caught a glimpse of her ruined wrists with their ugly slashes grinning like perverse stigmata, he felt remorse, but this was quickly replaced with acid anger. The torturer had now become the tortured. 'Would you have killed yourself for me? For da or Timmy? No. Just a phoney redneck who lost his scabby leg to a fish.' He saw movement in her eyes' lids. 'Yes, that's right, a rotten fish like you get down in Charley Wilson's.'

Slowly, her exhausted eyes appeared from behind the curtains of her lids. Her eyes had turned dark, the way a beetle's eyes appear against a raindrop. 'Promise you'll tell nobody about Mister Costa . . . his leg,' she begged, gripping his hand tight with what little strength she possessed. 'Please . . .'

'Why? Afraid people will laugh, make jokes about your great hero?'

'It would kill your father, if he knew what I've done. Promise me, Dominic. Please . . .'

A taste entered his mouth at that exact moment, a taste of watered metal, the post-taste of the dentist drill, the altered taste of vengeance, as if his anger had melted his skull, filtering it down through his nose and mouth.

He shook his head. 'I'm not goin' to lie – not for you, *never* for you. It's not dad you're worried about. Is it?'

'Promise me . . .'

Before he could reply, his father came to the side of the bed, his voice full of cardboard confidence. 'The doctor says you're coming along fine, my dear, but that you really need to start eating, to help build your strength.'

Resentfully, she closed her eyes, closing out the image of him standing there, so helpful and caring, so pathetically predictable.

'When you get out, things will be better. I promise, Julia.' He attempted a smile, hoping she would open her eyes. 'I'm thinking of applying for another job, one nearer to home. I know it hasn't been easy for you managing the house, the children . . .' The words were coming out awkwardly as he sat down, next to the bed, silently chained to the guilt of invested memories that were cemented in the heat of anger and fury. He would always love her, be eternally grateful for her acceptance of him. She meant everything to him – always would.

Dominic wanted to scream, to tell him to stop apologising. She was the one who should be on her knees, not him.

Angry and needing to get away, Dominic left the ward,

quickly taking the back-stairs two at a time. The stairway was rarely used and the lighting was faint and eerie fanning his shadow into four separate beings.

Halfway down, he thought he heard something, not too far behind as a terrible feeling told him that the exit door would be barred and nailed, laughing at him, forcing him back up the stairs to where the strange sounds waited.

He ran at the door with every dot of strength left in his body. He would run right through the door, if need be, smashing it into sawdust and toothpicks. He would destroy it, kick it, laugh at –

He went through the unlocked door with ease, landing on his arse, the soft muck cushioning it but not his embarrassment.

As he pushed himself up, he saw four figures wave at him from the grubby windows of the hospital, indicating for him to come back in, have a wee chat. They looked like Kane and Nutter and Joey Maxwell. The smallest of the four stood in front, smiling sadly. It was Larkin's mother. Her lips were moving, mouthing unheard words.

Dominic ran faster, feeling her eyes on his back. They were like tiny bats coming after him hoping to suck his blood. 'Fuck off! Fuck off! Fuck off!' he screamed, running, running, running, northbound like a freight train on a slippery track.

It was quite by accident that he found himself walking close to Dakota's – at least that was what he told himself. Smoke was coming from the chimney, but other than that, there was little sign of life.

He wondered what she was doing right now, in that terrible looking place. Eating? Laughing? Did she ever think about him? He doubted it. 'I shouldn't have returned.'

He thought he could hear voices, almost in a whisper, so he turned to leave, just as his eye caught sight of the barn. She was in there. He knew it, painting her ticket out of this shitty town, preparing herself for the fame that was hers for the taking.

The barn door squeaked loudly and Dominic cursed it as he slithered into the safety of shadows and lumpy shapes covered in dusty linen. He wondered which shape – if any– hid his portrait, and his heart beat a fraction faster with hope as he inched his way forward.

From the corner of his eye a tiny red glow faded in and out of the shadows and fractured light. He turned to see its source, his eyes trying desperately to focus in the impossible darkness.

'Private ground. Trespassin' gets you killed.' The voice startled him but he managed to say the word "shit" before his mouth froze with fear.

A woman, her face sheltered from the light, stood in the doorway as she sucked on a cigarette, its hot nipple glowing ghostly, like an SOS message at sea.

She had a shotgun housed in the crank of her elbow, cradling it affectionately like a sleeping child. It was an ugly-looking weapon, speckled with tiny freckles of rust that teased out the metal into an uneven surface. Dominic had never set eyes on her before, but there was little doubt in his spinning head that this was the legend; this was Dakota's mother.

'What's your business snoopin' about my property?'

A million lies raced through his head, but his tongue became wood and refused to acknowledge any of them. His stomach was making strange noises and he held the cheeks of his arse, tight, terrified of its possible action.

'I was . . . searchin' for a friend of mine. Larkin's his name. I thought I saw him head this way, but I must've been mistaken.'

She grinned. 'Your eyes do a strange twitchin' when you're lyin', even in the dark. Did you know that? Larkin's the boy who murdered his mother, the junkie. Isn't he? He's also the one who destroyed my daughter. So what would he be doin' in my place?' She moved the shotgun, pointing it directly at Dominic's groin. 'I think you should come along into the house until I figure what's to be done with you . . . Dominic.'

The smile that appeared on her face was a carbon copy of

Dakota's the day she almost drowned him. Liquid was seeping through into his pants as he wondered how in hell she knew his name. His only hope was of seeing Dakota, waiting there, as they entered the darkness of the house. He would beg her to save him.

They entered through the scullery which smelt of stale paint and decaying potatoes. Unwashed pots formed a metallic pyramid in the sink. A block of butter, touched by heat, had turned to mush.

'Sit yourself down, over there,' she said, pointing the shotgun at a corner.

To Dominic's relief, she placed the weapon on a nail attached to the wall before sitting down, opposite him, on an old sofa.

Flames from the half-dead fire lit up the room, eerily turning everything into slow motion. He was terrified to look at her face, but he couldn't resist the magnetic attraction it had.

Her black hair was pulled back so tight her skull must have hurt. Her eyes were almost as dark but there was a gleam reflecting in them; tiny blue gleams that had a life of their own. But it was the smile on her face that unsettled him most, the same angry upturned lip that belonged to her daughter, and just like her daughter there was no doubting the nastiness lurking, waiting to leap and slash at an unsuspecting victim.

Directly above her head, a sepia-coloured moth was trapped in a web, its large wings spread open like unwrapped sweetie paper. In the web's background, a rustic setting of other moths littered the silky kite-like autumn leaves hiding from the wind. It made him think of the flies in Fleming's greengrocer shop, dangling on the ceiling, pulling wings apart.

The woman did not speak, simply stared at him, as if she knew the power a perfect measure of silence had, its threatening actuality and ruthlessness, how it manipulates the mind into seeing things, making it believe the impossible.

Fear began to play tricks with his eyes, the raw feeling of fear which only isolation can produce. One moment she was

Dakota, smiling, telling him all would be fine, it had all been a terrible mistake, then the next moment the mother was back, telling him there would be no leaving – at least not while he lived.

Softly, the silence in the room was interrupted. It was only now that he heard the strange noises coming from somewhere near, somewhere beside him.

Soft squeals of fear filled the room.

The squeals became louder, more numerous, as if permission had been granted by some strange command, as if they were warning him to flee, make a run for it while he could.

What seemed an eternity ended by the woman's movements as she reached and revealed the source of those horrible tiny sounds of fear and dread.

'Hares. Don't you just love them when they make that sound of complete hopelessness.' It was a statement, not a question, as she pulled the squealing creature unceremoniously by the ears from a large trap stationed at her side. The creature made the sound a hungry baby makes searching for a nipple: a haunting sound so ominous it reached to the ghetto of Dominic's soul, tattooing it forever.

Expertly, she held the struggling hare inches from his mesmerised face, its whiskers nervously capturing dust motes when, with sleight-of-hand, she produced a pearl-handled knife and, to his shock – but puerile fascination – slit the animal's throat, releasing a leaf of blood that covered her fingernails like rose petals.

Dominic's hands moved instinctively to his throat.

Over the next few hours, twenty hares met a similar fate. The mercuric bluish entrails, which slipped through her fingers like crimson sand, were deposited into a tin bucket. The skins, festooned upon the walls and resembling leaves of tobacco, retained their tiny faces, each adorned with grotesque, posthumous grins. Pity and wonder emoted from the scene, and there, in the midst of the bloody slaughter, Dominic came of age with the knowledge that life is arbitrary to a fickle God who alone understands the esoteric incongruity of life and death with their seamless, paradoxical confluence.

'Don't pay them no heed,' advised the woman, watching Dominic's eyes skim over the dead. 'They're only animals; nothin' but simple animals.' She wiped the sweat from her face leaving a trail of skidded blood on her mouth. The blood glazed her lips, making them fat and obscene, as she came to the last of the kill.

Swiftly, she cut, almost ear-to-ear, before dangling the carcass in front of his face. 'Stick your finger in its throat,' she whispered, her voice hypnotising, just like her daughter's.

'I . . . I can't,' he mumbled, his entire body soaked with sweat. He wanted to vomit.

'But you have. Haven't you?' said her voice. '*Do it.*'

Gingerly, he complied, placing a shaking finger in the bloody gap that had once been the hare's throat.

'What does it feel like, *Dom-in-ic?*' she asked, cutting his name up, as if she were slicing bread.

The hare still kicked for the life that was gone and tiny drops of its blood dripped on his hand.

The fool in him didn't see the trap she had set and he gladly answered, hoping it would buy his freedom. 'Sticky . . . warm.'

'Warm? Sticky? Is that how my daughter felt, you little whore master, stickin' your filthy cock in her, gettin' it for free?' She wiped the blood-stained knife on her skirt. 'Let me tell you somethin', just this once, *Dom-in-ic*. I've been lookin' after my daughter since the day she came out of me, all covered in shit and blood, and she certainly needs no knight in shittin' armour to come to her rescue,' she whispered, shoving the dead creature into his face, twisting it violently, soaking him with its blood and flapping skin. 'There is nothin' in this world for free, *Dom-in-ic*. Payment must be made. Always.'

The taste of animal flooded his mouth. He could taste it, like a disease simmering in sickness. Tiny needles of pain began to burn his skull and he knew he was about to die when she reached for the shotgun, placing it tight to his face, forcing it to his skin, touching his aching jawbones. A strange chill shot through his bones and went up the side of his face, causing him to shiver.

She cocked the weapon, yet all he could do was hold his breath and wait. There would be no time for praying, but he thought about Heaven and Hell, wondering which one would accept him. He wondered if Joey Maxwell would meet him; he hoped Kane wouldn't.

'If you ever come back here – you'll be the hare. Do I make myself clear, *Dom-in-nic?*'

He willed his lips to move, but no sound came.

'Well, *Dom-in-ic?*' She pushed the weapon tighter against his skin.

He nodded.

'Good.' She removed the filthy weapon from his face, leaving two perfect circles of red on his skin, made by the barrels. 'I *will* use it, *Dom-in-ic*. No ifs, ands or buts. Don't ever let me see you again, not here, not near my daughter – ever!'

Like a drunk let loose, he staggered backwards from the room, into the night air filled with gossiping insects and their orchestral hum of wings, elated to be alive, yet full of the shame of a rape victim. Somehow he had brought this on himself. He deserved every tiny knot of pain and humiliation squeezing throughout his body.

Overhead, the sky's was ugly and gorgeous, like a salmon gutted to the neck, its entrails spilling as he ran for freedom. Everything began to spin. The trees became a blur while the grinning moon floated merrily above, exposing him with its giant spotlight of righteousness, allowing the world to see what a fool he had been.

'I told you not to come back, but you wouldn't listen. You really are stupid, Dominic. Stupid beyond belief,' said Dakota, pulling him into the barn.

Twenty-one

He could only hear her movement as nothing but darkness pressed against him, but the relief was tremendous. It made him feel alive.

'Where are you, Dakota? Is this another one of your games? Hide and seek?' He could hear the sound of tiny fibres breaking, as if someone was walking on brittle straw.

An indiscernible movement – distinguishable only by its textured shape – helped focus his eyes.

'Why don't you answer me?' he asked, moving slowly towards the shape. 'I never thought I would see the day when you'd be scared of me.'

'And you never will, Dominic,' responded her uncharacteristically soft voice.

'Turn on the lights,' he asked, knowing he was in touching range.

'No. Let's keep it like this – at least for a little while longer.'

He could smell her body smells of soap and other dizzyingly wonderful smells that reminded him of the happiest time of his life, alone with her, touching her, wanting her.

'You lied. Didn't you?' he accused. 'You told me you loved me.'

'Love?' replied Dakota, contemptuously. 'Just like real friends – there is no such thing. Remember, I told you that once before? I never loved you – never loved anyone. I never once told you I loved you, did I? You believed too much in your own imagination. That was always your problem, believin' in things that never existed, like love and magic, abracadabra and hocus-pocus.' She turned on a light and the barn lit up. 'Could you love this, my Dominic?'

He froze, unable to move, not believing what his eyes told him, not believing the mangled face before him was that of Dakota's.

'Oh, Dakota . . .' He wanted to die. 'Who did this to you?'

'Why? What would you do, Dominic? Kill him? I doubt it very much,' she sneered, bringing her face closer. 'Well? Would you?' The rips in her face were raw, seemingly held in concert by filthy, amateurish bandages. 'Gorgeously cruel, don't you think?'

'I . . . I . . . don't know what I can do, Dakota, to help. Tell me.'

'You? You help me?' she shook her head, disgusted with him. 'Actually, I've become quite fond of them. They will be there for me, always.'

Foolishly, he let words flow from his mouth, words he immediately regretted. 'If only I knew magic, Dakota. I mean real magic.'

'Magic? You want magic, Dominic? Well, I present to you the greatest magic show you will ever see. Kaleidoscopic distortions of reality from all our dreams, all our pains and nails hammered into our hands.' Quickly, she removed three covers. 'The greatness of any paintin' is measured by its ability to keep surprisin', revealin' somethin' new each time we go back to look at it. I'm sure you'll agree, Dominic, there are many surprises to be found in my work.'

An enormous canvas titled *An Effigy of Calvary* took centre stage. It depicted crucified scarecrows barking at the moon. Barbed wire squeezed out purple blood from each ragged face, spilling down, forming a puddle, shaped uncannily like the town.

The second painting was titled *Still Life* and evoked a similar unnerving feeling with its portrayal of an abortion, decapitated by a piano string. The child's face was fully developed, beautiful, its eyes terrifyingly real.

But it was the last painting which mesmerised, as it sucked Dominic into its beautiful, yet repulsive theme of animals – pigs – mating, watched by a goddess, herself comprised of animal and insect parts. It was a mosaic tapestry of exoticness, and simply called *Man*, despite the fact that the painting's central character was obviously a woman. The nude's butterfly-shaped ears protruded from black, cascading hair, partly covering a field mouse, its nose twitching with delight. Even the breasts were capped with elegiac, puppy-dog eyes while a shadowy mound of hair resting between the nude's legs was, in fact, a tarantula, its hairy legs wrapped menacingly around a bloody, severed phallus-shaped mushroom. The spider seemed to stalk the canvas, as if it were ready to leap.

Groups of pigs mated in the painting's background, aroused by the nude. The pigs' faces had grotesque, almost human similitude.

Dominic's heart beat faster, as his eyes scanned the pigs. He tried to resist, but it was useless. The pigs were calling him, whispering his name. *Dominic. Dominic. Dominic.* It sounded like a Gregorian chant. They wanted him to join them. *Dominic. Dominic. Dominic. Come and join the fun,* said a sow, smiling so lovingly it was incredible to behold. A boar stood over the sow, ready for mounting her, its large lance-like penis erect for battle. The boar appeared to be winking at him, granting him permission to mount the sow first. *Take her. She's yours, Dominic. One good fuck, if I say so myself . . .*

'Oh, God . . .' Dominic felt his stomach move as he noticed the missing leg on the boar.

'What? You don't like my paintings, Dominic?' asked Dakota, feigning hurt. 'But you yourself told me she sounded like a pig when he stuck it in her. All that gruntin', her and Mister One-leg. Oink oink!' She was smiling that horrible smile she kept for special moments such as this.

The feeling of *déjà vu* pulsated through his body. He imagined himself back at the junkyard, smashing a skull to a pulp, its eye almost popping out.

'You're sick – very sick. I need to get out of here, away from you,' he whispered, sweat soaking his skin. He was frightened of what he was now capable of doing to her.

'Oh, you can go, my gentle Dominic. I told you a long time ago that I didn't need you. I used you, just like I used Larkin to kill Kane.' She could see his hurt, his confusion, and she relished it.

'Larkin killed Kane because of me,' said Dominic, not believing a single word from her mouth. 'He knew how much I hated Kane, even though I didn't – not in the way he thought.'

'For you?' She shook her head.

He wished she would stop smiling. It made her ugly. It made him want to do something to get rid of the ugliness, restore the beauty.

'Larkin killed for one reason and one reason only – I asked him. He would never have killed for you. Not in a million years.'

'You asked him? I don't believe you. You're lyin'. You're good at that. Very good and nasty.'

'I know you killed Nutter, Dominic. Your best *friend* told me all about it.'

Dominic felt an invisible punch hit him in the centre of his stomach as he watched her terrible eyes and mouth with their exquisite nastiness of shadows flickering inches from his face, taunting him.

'It took Larkin a while to realise how you mistakenly thought he killed Kane because you didn't like him – ha! How we laughed at that. The little mouse had become a great lion, all for a mistake. All you did by killin' Nutter was to prove to Larkin that he really did have the Power. It was the Power, not you, that had saved his life. You were just the tool he used.'

'You're lyin'.'

'I don't care what you believe, but I will make you believe, this last time. And once you believe, you will know for always just how little you meant to me – how little you meant to any of us.' Again, the broken-bottle-in-your-face smile appeared, the one that flayed his skin.

She sat down on a battered box, opposite him, scanning his face with her eyes, recording every movement of bewilderment on it.

'Kane used to come to see this mother once a week. He was addicted to her – just like you were to me. The only difference between you and him was that he had to pay for what you got free.' She watched his face flush, loving the hurt in it. 'When he was done with her, he would come to the little girl's room, forcin' himself on top of her like the disgustin' pig he was. The mother was in self-denial. "Kane would do no such thing", she assured herself when the little girl told her. "He was a gentleman, kind with his money." ' Dakota's voiced suddenly seemed tired, drained. 'When his wife died, Kane's visits became daily, his attacks on the little girl more brutal. She would be sketchin' nervously at the window, waitin' for him to arrive. She could hear her mother's false laughter from downstairs as a remarkable nothingness slowly touched her while she listened to the footsteps soundin' up the stairs. Each footstep he took sounded in her chest, like a hammer tryin' to smash it. The little girl tried to pretend she was invisible, tryin' to ignore the yellow grin on his face as it peeped sneakily from behind the door. "Put that shit away and get ready" he would whisper as the room closed in on her. She couldn't breathe. Would no one help her?

Do they hate her that much? She knew they could hear her. Please. Someone, somewhere, help her. But no one ever listened. They must mind their own business. They have books full of excuses. Even their God needs shut-eye when it suits him.'

In spite of the feeling of revulsion, the uninterrupted flow of monologue held Dominic spellbound with its story of family intrigue, dirty dealing and sexual madness.

'The little girl can still see him, every night, undoin' his belt buckle, allowing his greasy trousers to slide down his bony, hairy legs . . .'

Dominic could see her shudder and reached to touch her.

'*Don't!*' she hissed, eyes glistening with rage. 'I haven't even told you about the mother, yet, the kind and gentle mother with her sewin' basket. "Do you want me to stitch it up!" she howled, pushin' the needle into the little girl's naked front. "If I sew up your purse you will have to pee out your bum! Is that what you want? All the children laughin' at you and calling you pee in the bum? Well! Answer me!" The little girl was so terrified she wet herself. "That's your Pandora's box. Open it, and every conceivable evil will be released. Demons and devils with great bloody wings will take you away. Is that what you want, you little harlot? Is it!" The mother shook the little girl. "All men are evil – *all* men. No exceptions. Make them pay with money and pain." The little girl managed to pull away from the grip, but not before the mother warned her that she would check her underwear each and every month for the tiny map of blood that would prevent the demons from coming for her and God help her if the magic map wasn't there.' Dakota stared directly into his eyes. 'You see, the little girl learned a lot from them . . .'

Dominic remained silent. He felt exhausted, mentally and physically, drained of all emotion.

'I don't want any of you to touch me again – ever,' continued Dakota. 'I thought I could depend on you to kill Kane, punish him for what he did to me. But I was mistaken, you were useless, interested in only one thing, just like the rest of the animals. You killed Nutter for a so-called friend who laughed at you, yet you couldn't kill Kane for what he did to me, and you claimed to love me? You were weak, so weak . . .'

'You never told me about Kane. How could I do anythin'? I was terrified of him, also.'

'I quickly realised you wouldn't have done a thing. You are a coward. Weak. You will always be Chicken Boy.'

'And Larkin? He killed his mother. But it was you who did that. Didn't you? Fucked with his head, just like you did with mine. It was you who planted the seed,' said Dominic, shaking his head with disgust.

Dakota thought for a moment. 'Perhaps. Perhaps it would have come sooner or later. Perhaps the seed only needed a little watering. Larkin was different – at the beginnin'. I was jealous of his strength, and allowed that jealousy to cloud my judgement of him. I didn't want to admit to myself that he was as strong as me – perhaps stronger. His darkness was his strength, those horrible scars on his face, those terrible thoughts in his head, poundin' away in his skull. I showed him how to thrive on them, not reject them. But in the end, he became weak, wantin' me, just like you wanted – and still want – me. I thought he was different, but none of you are. The smell of a woman drives you all mad. It can even make you kill.' She smiled. 'All it took was the taste of my breast, Dominic. Can you believe how weak he was, in the end? A breast, a hardened piece of fat, and he would kill for it. I let him suck on it, just like I let you suck on it, soothin' him with words his mother never spoke to him, words he had always wanted to hear. And as he sucked like a greedy little piglet I told him that I was the mommy now, and he would be my obedient son.'

Dominic wanted to close his ears. 'You're evil and sick.'

'I know, and you loved every sick and evil moment of being with me. You had security from my evil, followin' and being dominated by someone stronger. I was your Pied Piper, and don't deny how much you loved every minute of it.' She removed something from a top shelf, and shoved it into his chest. 'Here. This will tell you all about your friend.' It was a green folder.

Before Dominic could say a word, she kicked open the barn door. 'Now, get out. As my mother said, don't come back. You won't be let off so easily if you make that mistake. She *will* kill you.'

There is a class of occurrences so far from the norm they become surreal, residing in their own realty, occupying where the improbable is commonplace and this was what he was experiencing as he held his breath for what seemed an eternity, waiting for the silence of the night to return. He walked for hours, aimlessly, thinking about nothing but that night in the junkyard when he killed to save Larkin's life and to repay a terrible debt. If Dakota spoke the truth, he'd never had the debt. He had become a murderer for nothing.

With these thoughts, he seemed to succumb to the realms of oblivion. He could fall right into it and be carried away, everlastingly, freed from life's oppressive deepness and all the dark guilt that clings stubbornly to the soul.

The rainy streets were empty, except for a few vehicles. A car halted on the red and he could see its wipers scything the windscreen leaving iridescent ellipses in their wake.

Tomorrow, he would return to school. Nutter would be there, demanding his dinner money. Larkin would be waiting after school, smoking a cigarette, grinning, ready to take him to *Gino's* for *Coke* and chips. Old Kane would still slap him on the head, hard, for nothing. But Dominic wouldn't complain. In fact, he would welcome it. It would be proof – not that he needed it – that this nightmare had never really happened. Any minute now and he would wake up, screaming to his mother that Timmy had done it again: pissed all over him.

He remained motionless. Not breathing. Not thinking.

Somewhere in the distance he could hear a siren, the sound of an ambulance. Soon there would be no sound at all, just ghosts feasting on memories of the dead in an echo of nothingness and unforgiving torment.

He wanted to cry, but the ghosts wouldn't let him. Not now. Not ever.

Epilogue

Rats scurried quickly into holes as Larkin approached the perimeter wall of the prison. Within minutes of arriving, Dominic sat across from a face he thought he would never see again.

Larkin reached out his hand and Dominic shook it. Larkin didn't speak, simply stared with those eyes that terrified, with that face that had been the last face ever seen by many of his victims.

After all these years, Dominic couldn't think of one word to say and quickly fumbled for the tape recorder bulging in his pocket, placing it between them and the seriousness of business unfinished.

'Do you have a problem with this?' he asked, hitting the "record" button.

There was hate in Larkin's eyes; not original hate but the secretive, retrospective hate anchored in memory. He seemed to be finding it difficult to control himself.

Dominic wondered if he was deliberately goading Larkin, or

if it was something subconscious, something that now came naturally to him as a reporter.

'Turn that off,' said Larkin, so softly Dominic barely heard him. 'Never forget who I am. Now, ask my permission.'

Dominic felt his face burning. 'I thought I did. May I turn this on?'

Larkin grinned. 'No . . . not yet. First, tell me what's it's like for you, finally realizin' one of your dreams. Was it worth it?'

Dominic could hear seagulls and crows squawking outside, fighting over discarded garbage and dead things.

'Was what worth it?' he eventually replied, focusing on Larkin's face but not seeing it. 'This? Leavin' all this glory behind? God, no! Look what I've missed.' There was bitterness in his voice and he had suddenly become defensive, justifying his actions, as if they needed to be justified.

Larkin was attempting to reverse the roles, as if he were the reporter and Dominic the subject. Smiling, he reached over and pushed down on the "record" button bringing it to life. 'You know your mother always waited for your return, told whole town you'd be back. But you didn't come, did you – at least not while she lived. Did you hate her that much? You wouldn't come back for her funeral but you came back for my death. Is that ironic or just perverse?'

Larkin's perception was as keen as ever. His words – like himself – took no prisoners. Dominic was conscious of the tape's whispery whirl. At any moment it would release itself, cut his throat. Larkin was daring him to turn it off, hoping to tease out the words that sat in his throat like stones covered in dust.

'Killin' for a livin',' he continued. 'That would make a great headline for your readers. Don't you think?' He smiled before leaning back on his chair. 'The first is the worst and, strangely, the best. Let me explain the contradiction. Doubt, fear – religion even – they all play a part. Initially, it eats away at you, until the second killin' comes along. That helps, a bit, because it muddles the first, slightly. The third? Even better, because by then, you've forgotten the first time, practically, almost like a crack addict. But it's a lot easier to obtain a fix. People are such a cheap commodity.'

Larkin stopped speaking, permitting the power of emptiness to sit between them, as if it were a judge that had listened intently to each spoken word and whose testimony would come later.

He lit a cigarette before continuing. The match's angry head filled the room with sulphur. 'But of course, you may have an entirely different perspective. Perhaps you would like to indulge in some youthful . . . sin. But first, shouldn't you turn the tape off. Wouldn't want all your fancy friends knowin' too much about their Dominic, would we?' He blew smoke into the air.

Dominic said nothing. He could erase and censor the tape later. Let Larkin's mouth continue, unabated. It would unwittingly strengthen Dominic's position at the newspaper. His name would be remembered for a long time.

Larkin continued on, relentlessly, as if every second of his life must be recorded. Finally, almost an hour later, he slumped back in his chair, exhausted, like a boxer who had just completed the fight of his career. And when Dominic said nothing, simply returning the stare, Larkin angrily spat out the last few words in his throat. 'You're no better than me, knowin' the necessity that unexpectedly forces a person, in a split second, to be judge and jury. Blood is all over your hands. Just like mine.'

Dominic turned the tape recorder off, and stood. Larkin was a stranger now, yet familiar too, in the frightening way when the past that you so desperately want to forget suddenly comes clawing back in front of your eyes.

'No, you're wrong,' said Dominic, pocketing the tape recorder. 'We *are* opposites. Every day, since it happened, I have tried to erase that terrible night from my brain. But like a stubborn, bloody stain, it refused to budge. But I think, in your own sick way, you have helped me to finally come to terms with what I did.'

Dominic left the room to the sound of Larkin's accusing voice reverberating and echoing off the black and silver glass.

The plane took off and he glanced back at the town as lights came on in every home, softly, slowly turning into sparkling black and silver rhinestones. A tourist or a stranger would love it. So welcoming. But like a beautiful marble mausoleum, it wasn't until you looked inside, finding the horror of its contents, that you would realise you were trapped.

Dominic could still see the eerie glow of the prison below him and pictured Larkin sitting, watching the sky, following the plane with those terrible eyes, fooling himself that he had the power to make it crash. Thoughts camped in his head questioning what had been, what had yet to be, and the contradictory bonding of guilt and clear conscience which had already started to fuse into a repetitive oneness, threatening to suffocate him.

It was then that he made the decision. There would be no erasing of the tape. It would be kept, in its entirety, for all to hear. Let them judge. He had judged himself, had punished himself over and over again. He was heading home – home to where he belonged. In just two weeks Larkin would face his executioner and Dominic would be "free".

A few minutes later, the town disappeared in the darkness of night clouds and a great expanse that suddenly let go. To his right, the sky's canopy began to cover the moon, carpeting everything below in a dull quietness, like the hum of a light bulb just extinguished in the stillness of the night's shadow. He sat back in his seat and closed his eyes and suddenly everything felt loose. *I am going home*, he told himself, *and no amount of magic will change that. Ever.*

Autumn 2003

A MEMOIR

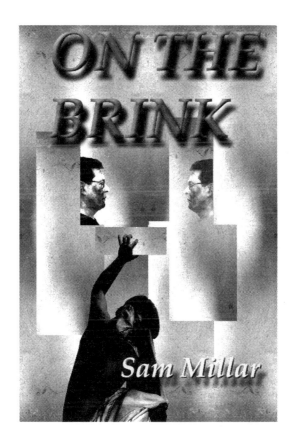

ISBN: 0-9542607-7-5

Wynkin deWorde